Table of Contents

The sound of wind rattling the window frames, woke Lilly out of a deep sleep. She could hear the sounds and struggled to keep her eyes shut but her young mind had already started pulling her into consciousness.

Lilly

She heard a woman whisper her name.

Lilly

Lilly opened her eyes and looked around. The room was dark and small, consisting of a bed and a small dresser. The door to the remainder of the room was open and beyond, nothing but black.

She couldn't remember if she had shut the door on not. But now, it was open and she had no choice but to go back to sleep or shut it.

Someone called out my name.

Lilly felt a chill go down her spine. She knew that it was best to remain in place, lying in bed and just wait for morning. But something was pulling her out of bed, gently guiding her across the floor, and leading her to the window that overlooked the back of the hotel.

Outside, the world was dark and wet. Raindrops splattered against the glass, and the trees lining the perimeter of the hotel swayed to and fro in an insane dance only possible due to the ferocity of Mother Nature.

Suddenly, Lilly saw a black figure standing on the ground near the trees. At first, she thought it might be her imagination, and given what she'd heard next door only to find out that no one was there—made her wonder if she could trust any of her senses … however, the figure went from a solid black to having a shape and a face.

There's a woman down there! What is she doing outside in the rain?

A feeling of warmth started in Lilly's feet and slowly spread along her legs, traveling up her body. It was an uncomfortable sensation and for a brief moment she worried that she had wet her pants. It spread up her neck and then along her head, permeating her mind with a foggy heat that shut out all reason.

Come to me, Lilly.

THE INN

&

OTHER DARK TALES

by Sara Brooke

THE INN

1

The darkness was complete and hung over the vast landscape, covering it with a finality that removed any essence of welcoming. It wound its way around the trees that lined the narrow two-lane highway, and covered the rest of the surrounding forests for as far as the eye could see.

Denise Paskins gripped the steering wheel tightly, trying to keep her eyes on the road. The hurricane, now a Category 4 storm named Slate, was barreling through the Atlantic, with a direct hit on Miami Beach in its sights. Denise lived near the water in a two-bedroom apartment. She had no choice but to evacuate once the Mayor announced that Zone A would have to leave due to the potential of massive storm surge.

Her destination was a simple countryside hotel in north Georgia, about an hour away from Atlanta. Website photos revealed a clean, simple place with low nightly rates. With nothing available for miles, Denise had booked it immediately, feeling relieved and ready to evacuate.

But the drive on the turnpike had been long and exhausting, fighting wall-to-wall traffic, and her ten-year-old daughter Lilly was on a tear, asking questions non-stop.

"Mom, will the storm hit us?"

"Mom, when will we be there?"

"Mom, can I have more beef jerky?"

Denise wondered if she would make it. They had stopped at a simple barbeque restaurant and despite the break giving her a slight respite from the drive; she was feeling the weight of the travels on her shoulders.

And now, she was in the middle of nowhere, trying to navigate a road that wound through a never-ending forest. It was dark, and for some reason, the local department of transportation had chosen to forgo streetlights.

"Mom, it's really dark. When are we getting there?"

For fuck's sake. She's asked me that question a million times. Why can't she just take a nap? Don't ten-year-olds still take naps?

"Soon."

The road was not only narrow, but winding as well. Denise had to focus and slow down the car because the lines on the road were difficult to follow and vehicles driving in the other direction blinded her every time they passed by.

Her hands hurt from stiffly grasping the wheel, and she tried to flex each finger. She glanced quickly at the GPS and saw that there were only 20 minutes left for the drive.

Where is this place? I'm in the middle of nowhere. Haven't even seen a gas station in a while. There's no houses, no people, no light. Maybe I'll find another place in the morning.

But Denise knew that wasn't going to happen. She had searched TripAdvisor for nearly an hour trying to find a place to stay, and the Countryside Inn was the only place with available rooms. There were no other options.

"Mom, look! There is it!"

Lilly's voice cut through the air, and Denise jumped in her seat, momentarily losing control of the wheel. The car swerved into the other lane, and she fought to control the vehicle pulling on the wheel. Her foot eased off the gas pedal and the car returned to the proper lane, slowing down.

"Shit!"

Lilly giggled in the backseat. She loved hearing her mother curse and even the threat of an accident in the middle of the night couldn't take away from her glee.

Denise sighed loudly and looked at the yellowish sign to her right.

Countryside Inn

It was hard to see the hotel at first, and it was even more

difficult to find the entryway. Denise took a quick breath and slowed the car, turning it to the right. On each side of the road, large trees with piles of hanging moss stood like sentries, their arms reaching out toward the car as if it to grab it and swallow it whole.

Lilly was silent and for the first time in hours, wasn't trying to be a backseat driver. She was suddenly very nervous and wasn't entirely sure why.

As Denise began to drive down a slender, paved path, the hotel finally came fully into view. It was colonial styled and the white columns in the front of the building stood in stark contrast to the surrounding darkness. A few rocking chairs lined the porch, and byzantine windows with stained glass were spaced out along the wall, adding to the strange look of the building.

The upstairs windows were more standard in style, but there was still something odd about the inn. And then, Denise realized what it was.

There was only light downstairs. Upstairs, all the windows were dark.

Maybe they've closed the shades?

Denise wondered if the inn was empty. A gust of wind struck the car and reminded her that a hurricane was threatening and many people were evacuating.

We can't be the only ones. There's got to be other people who found this place on the internet.

Denise guided the car into a parking spot beside the building and finally saw the sign.

Country Side Inn – A Hotel for Weary Travelers

"Mom, it doesn't look like there's anyone in there," Lilly said, her voice wavering.

"I'm sure there's people inside. Let's go in and get our room. Don't forget to grab your suitcase."

As soon as Denise opened her car door, a gust of wind swept around her and she felt a gentle mist against her skin. It was warm and uncomfortable.

"Come on, let's go inside quickly. The weather here isn't good," she instructed Lilly.

"Ok, ok."

Lilly grunted and pulled her small suitcase from the backseat.

Denise opened the trunk and pulled her suitcase out. It was heavy and filled with things that she knew she probably didn't need.

Shutting the trunk, Denise turned around and stared at the hotel. The wind was whipping up around them and had begun to emit a low howl. Still, she stared at the building in front of them as if in a trance.

Why are all the windows dark? This place doesn't seem right. Maybe we should just turn around and go look for another place to stay. But the woods out here are so dark, and there's no street signs anywhere. I'm not sure this is such a good idea.

"Mom, it's windy out here! Let's go inside!"

"Alright, honey. Sorry, I must just be a little tired. Let's go."

But Denise couldn't shake the foggy feeling that had entered her mind and it remained with her as they carried their luggage, mounted the steps and opened the front door.

As they entered the building, a bell jangled above them. Denise was relieved to see that the foyer was well lit and the room felt comfortably warm. She was surprised that they hadn't seen more light from outside the inn, but pushed the thought out of her mind.

A slender elderly woman, with gray hair cut in a straight bob, stood behind the counter. She had kind eyes and put them immediately at ease.

"Why, hello there! Hope y'all didn't have a tough time getting here. The roads are pretty crappy this time of night, and the weather keeps getting worse. Just saw on the news that the storms' hitting down south but we seem to be getting some lousy stuff up here too."

Denise looked over at Lilly who seemed to be transfixed on the woman's face. She didn't blame her daughter for that reaction, because the warmth emanating from both the inn keeper and the lights inside were completely different than the atmosphere outside. Still, it was a welcome difference.

"Hi. Yes, it was a rough drive. I'm Denise Paskins and this is my daughter, Lilly. We have a reservation for tonight."

The inn keeper looked down at a pile of paper in front of her and sifted through it. "That's right. The Paskins family. I have your reservation right here." And she poked the paper with her finger as if to highlight that point.

Doesn't she have a computer? I hope she has a way to take down my credit card information.

As if reading her mind, the woman smiled, "Do you have a credit card and form of ID, please? And I'm Bonnie by the way. Don't hesitate to call down to me if you need anything." As she took Denise's card, she ran it through a manual credit card machine and continued talking. "Breakfast is served downstairs in the main dining room from six to nine. And then we get ready for lunch that starts at noon. But if you get hungry in the meantime, you can come down and see if the cook has left anything out. Usually, there's a plate of cookies or some leftover cake from dessert." She chuckled to herself. "It's not unusual for our guests to wake up in the middle of the night hungry for some sweets. I've got a hard time sleeping myself so if I'm up, I'll help myself to some of those delicious calories."

Bonnie handed the card back to Denise and nodded slowly. "You're in room six on the second floor. It's our larger suite and has an adjoining bedroom so that your daughter can be nearby. Here's the key."

Denise looked at the strange piece of metal that Bonnie had given her. It was designed in the shape of a clove with a wolf's head in the center. The rest of it looked like a skeleton key.

"Oh, I know it looks odd but that's the way the owners made the keys," Bonnie explained. "Back in the day when this inn was first built, there were stories about witches living in the surrounding woods, so the owners thought it would be quaint to design room keys with an insignia that resembled Wiccan beliefs."

"Oh." Denise wasn't sure what to say.

"It's ok, sweetie. Don't worry. The witches in the woods are just a myth. If you just stay indoors, keep your shades closed, and your door locked, they won't bother you."

Denise was about to say something else, when Bonnie burst into laughter, turned and left the counter. She went into a back office and closed the door.

"Mom, this place is weird."

This place is definitely weird.

Denise turned to get a better look at the foyer. Despite being called a "Countryside" Inn, there was nothing country-esque about the interior decorations. Large red curtains hung over the stained glass windows, velvet couches in a deep turquoise offered a gauche seating area and teardrop lights hung from the ceiling. On the walls, paintings of dark forests with threatening skies shared their ominous imagery, which wasn't so different from the growing storm outside.

"Ok, Lilly. Let's find the stairs and go to our room."

The stairwell was centrally located, but the steps were narrow and winding. Along the walls, faux candelabras sat in mini alcoves that were cut into the wall, making them feel as if they were ascending to a tower.

It was a macabre sight, and Denise decided immediately that in the morning they would look for another place to stay.

"Hey, Mom. There's our room! Look. Room six."

With hands that trembled slightly, Denise inserted the odd key into a hole underneath a brass door knob and the door clicked open smoothly. She took a deep breath and reached around for the wall, searching for a light switch—unwilling to go into the dark room. Her fingers connected to a basic switch, and she flicked it on, feeling vast relief when yellow-white light flooded the room.

Lilly giggled and went inside but before Denise entered Room Six, she looked back into the hallway. All the doors were closed and silence surrounded them.

It's not that late. Where are all the people here? Surely we're not the only ones staying in the inn. I should have asked Bonnie about that when we were checking in. Better remember to do that tomorrow morning.

The room was surprisingly luxurious. Each piece of furniture had been made from a dark oak, and looked in very good condition. The bed in one of the rooms was king-sized, and was adorned with a deep blue bedspread. The other in the adjoining bedroom was also a king bed and this one had an emerald green bedspread lying on it.

A small desk with an antique lamp was pressed up against one of the windows and a plasma-screen television was positioned in the middle of a large entertainment center that included a bar and numerous glass enclosures. These were empty, except for one that contained a metal sculpture with the same insignia as the key Bonnie had given them.

Two large bottles of water sat near the television.

After placing her suitcase down in the adjoining bedroom, Lilly took one of the water bottles and sat down on her mother's bed.

"Well, at least we get free water. But seriously Mom, this place is kind of weird. Do you think maybe we should find a more normal hotel? And where are all the people? It's really quiet in here. All you can hear is the wind outside."

Denise suddenly felt the exhaustion of the day press itself upon her shoulders. She rubbed her eyes and tried to give Lilly her most genuine smile. "I think you're right. This place was the only one available tonight. But first thing tomorrow, we will check out and look for some other place, ok? For right now, I need you to take a shower. I will take one after you, and then we can both go to bed."

Lilly groaned and nodded. "Ok, Mom. Why don't you take the first shower, and then I will take one after you. That way, we can go to bed as soon as I'm done."

She's such a sweet kid.

Denise smiled and ran her hands through Lilly's red mop of hair.

"Ok, let me go first and then it's your turn, young lady."

The bathroom was spacious and well-lit including a walk-in shower surrounded on all sides by glass paneling and shiny beige flooring. The spouts on the bathtub were golden wolves' heads and valves on each side indicated that the tub was also a spa.

If we had more time, I'd love to try out that bathtub, but Lilly's got to go to sleep.

The water felt wonderful as it cascaded down Denise's shoulders. The warmth of the spray eased some of the tension in her shoulders, and the soap bar the hotel had included smelled of wild berries. She stood under the torrents of water for a long time, thinking about her situation.

So, I'm not mother of the year. It would have been better if I could raise Lilly in a house that has more room instead of just two bedrooms. And Miami isn't the best place to raise a child. But our place is close to my work, so what am I supposed to do? I need to stop beating myself up about things. The divorce was hard. I lost half of my worth. And my loser ex-husband, who did nothing but spend our money during our entire marriage, walked away with half of all the money I made as a Marketing Director all these years. He doesn't even try to see Lilly regularly. And God forbid he even offer to help us during the storm. Shit, he has a three bedroom house in the suburbs with shutters and a generator.

She closed her eyes, feeling the water spill down between her shoulder blades.

It's probably better that I didn't stay with him anyway. The last thing I want to do is hunker down for a storm, surrounded by wild winds and torrential rains listening to him talk. He is such an idiot. Not sure why I stayed with him for all those years. A total mistake. Damn, I am so tired.

Denise realized that she had been standing in the shower for quite a while, and even though the water was still warm, she wanted to be sure to leave some for her daughter as well.

After she twisted the knob and turned off the water, Denise stood still for a moment.

Silence.

"Lilly, are you ok?"

No answer.

"Lilly, are you ready to take your shower?"

Still no answer.

Feeling her heart rate begin to increase, Denise quickly reached for a towel and grasped the soft white material, wrapping it quickly around her wrist. Trying hard to not panic, she dried off as best as possible, and then wrapped the towel around her torso.

As soon as she stepped out of the bathroom, Denise called out, "Lilly!"

Nothing. Just silence.

The room was empty.

Oh shit. Oh shit. Ok, just calm down. Let me put my pajamas on quickly, and I'll go find her. Can't be running around this strange hotel in just a towel.

Denise barely took a breath as she pulled pajama pants and a matching shirt out of her suitcase. Then, she turned and quickly threw open the door, staring wildly down the hallway and praying that her daughter hadn't been kidnapped.

2

As soon as the shower started, Lilly decided it was time to explore the bedroom. It was vast and had many drawers to open. She walked over to the entertainment center and opened the glass case that held the metal object with the wolf insignia.

It felt surprisingly light and cool on her palm. Suddenly, a wave of dizziness draped itself over her, and Lilly dropped the metal object on the ground. She staggered for a moment and then took a deep breath, feeling her body relax as the air escaped her lips.

She was about to lie down on her mother's bed when she heard the sound of a goat bleating. It was faint at first and then sounded louder.

An animal in the hotel? That can't be. It's impossible. No one is allowed to bring farm animals into a fancy hotel. How would they have gotten it up the stairs? That's impossible!

Lilly pressed her head to the wall and listened. She could hear people laughing in the other room and periodically, she would hear a goat bleat and then a rooster singing at the top of its lungs. The sound of water reminded her that her mother was in the shower, but she knew that this noise would keep them up for the rest of the night. So, she decided to go into the hallway, knock on the door and politely ask their neighbors to keep it down.

Lilly turned the knob on the door to their room and it opened slowly in front of her. The hallway was still lit and very bright, but now, it was silent. She was confused and tried to understand what was happening, but her young mind simply raced in circles without coming to a conclusion.

Stepping into the hallway, she could feel the plush carpet underneath her toes. It was beige with red spots that looked like flecks of blood.

I didn't notice that before. How did Mom and I not see that?

The room next door, Room Eight, looked identical from the outside. The door was simple oak with the words "Room Eight" engraved on a piece of metal that was affixed to the center.

With shaking hands, Lilly knocked on the door. The sound was hollow and reverberated throughout the hallway.

"Hello?" she asked. "Is anyone in there?"

It seemed to her as if the door moved just slightly and she was about to push on it, when she heard her mother's frantic voice pierce the silence.

"Lilly! What are you doing out here? You almost gave me a heart attack. I got out of the shower and you were gone!"

Her mother looked a mess. Wet hair stood up in all different directions and her eye makeup had dripped down her cheeks, given her a wild 80's punk rocker look.

Lilly looked back at the door to Room Eight and wondered how she was going to talk her way out of this situation.

"I don't understand. Roosters?"

For what seemed like the hundredth time, Lilly tried to explain to her mother what she'd heard in the room next door. It all sounded crazy, even to her, but she was desperate for her mother to believe her. Even though it was completely quiet now, she knew that what she'd heard through the walls hadn't been her imagination.

"I'm serious, Mom. There's some kind of wild party going on next door. I just know it. I wasn't hearing things."

"Honey, maybe they were just watching a movie next door and had the volume on too loud. Sometimes that can sound like it's real, but it is just something on TV."

Lilly shook her head violently. "No. It was real. Go over there, and knock on the door. You'll see there's something wrong."

Denise shook her head tiredly, and then glanced at her watch. "Ok. Here's what I'll do. I'll go next door and see if anyone answers. If not, I'm coming right back. Give me the key. I want you to stay here and not wander around. In fact, go ahead and lock the door after I leave. When I come back, I'll have the key and I can get in. But don't leave. You stay right here. Understand?"

"Yes, Mom."

Denise stood up and gave her daughter a hug. "I believe

you, but it's already ten o'clock at night and we both need to get some rest. So, let me deal with this and then we'll go to sleep."

Lilly watched as her mother slipped into her sandals, took the key and then left the room. She locked the door, and then sat on her mother's bed, fear taking over as she pulled the covers up over her knees.

3

Denise stepped into the hallway once more. The lights over-head were unnaturally bright, and the silence that hung in the air was nearly suffocating. She could hear herself breathing as she moved toward the room next door.

Reaching out she knocked on the door quickly.

This really doesn't feel right. I shouldn't be bothering these people so late at night. But Lilly doesn't usually tell lies. Something must have been going on for her to be so adamant.

"Fuck you, you cock sucking whore!"

The voice was so angry and violent that it frightened Denise immediately. And she wasn't sure if she'd heard properly, so she decided to be more diplomatic.

"I'm so sorry to bother you, and I know it's late. We were just wondering if you could turn down your television. My daughter said it was on a bit loud. It's quiet now, so I'm sorry to have disturbed you."

"Your mother sucked dick every night of her life. And you are a dirty, pig-loving, bitch!"

Now, Denise was angry. She couldn't understand why this person was being so vile. She was about to knock on the door again when she heard a screech that was so loud, she needed to cover her ears to block it out. Even after the screech stopped, the ringing in her ears continued for a brief moment.

She wondered if she should knock again, and decided it would be best to complain to the front desk. Looking back at her room, Denise considered calling but figured a face-to-face complaint might be best.

I'm sure Bonnie wouldn't stand for this. She'll help me.

The stairwell seemed steeper on the way down, but Denise took a deep breath and hurried down as quickly as she could—not wanting to loiter near the fake candles. She also wasn't entirely sure if the person in the room next door to her would be violent or try to hurt her, so it seemed that the faster she could enlist the help of someone else, the better.

When she reached the foyer, she looked around in confusion. The room looked different.

The green velvet couches were still there, along with the paintings on the wall, but it looked like everything had shifted somehow. The couches seemed to be in a more northerly position in the room and the painting of the woods was now on the wall behind the front desk, instead of by the couches as it had appeared when they'd arrived.

As for the reception desk—it was empty, and the hallway directly behind it was dark.

Denise walked up to the front and hit the bell, hoping that Bonnie was still awake. She waited a while and decided to hit the bell again.

When no one came back to the desk, Denise got a little bolder and looked at the papers on the desk. To her surprise, they didn't look like hotel receipts or paperwork at all. Instead, there were large symbols written on them in red ink and sentences of text that she couldn't understand.

Suddenly, a gust of wind hit the building and the lights flickered for a moment and then came back on.

"Can I help you with something?"

Denise nearly pissed in her pants at the sound of Bonnie's voice. She turned and saw that the innkeeper was standing at the desk, smiling and looking perfectly at ease.

Gathering her courage and trying not to look startled, Denise forced herself to sound calm. "Yes, I'm afraid we have a problem."

"I'm so sorry, what's wrong?"

Bonnie looked genuinely concerned, which made Denise feel better about asking for help.

"There's a very rude person in the room next door. First, they had their TV on very loud and then when we asked them to turn it down, they cursed me out."

The innkeeper looked dismayed and shook her head. "Well, Ms. Paskins, I'm very sorry about that. And believe me, I want to help you. But I can't. There's no one in Room Eight. In fact, many of our guests had to cancel tonight because the roads have become impassable near here due to flash flooding. So you're the only one on your floor tonight. That's how I was able to get you the best room on the floor."

Denise shook her head, "That's impossible. My daughter heard some very loud noises in the room next door, and I heard someone curse me out. I mean, the person was right near the door."

"Was it a man or woman?"

Denise tried to remember and realized that the voice had sounded androgynous. "I don't know. It was hard to tell."

Bonnie shook her head again and reached for a set of keys from under the desk. "Let me go upstairs and see what's going on. You can stay here, go to your room, or you can come with me. What would you prefer?"

The options were tricky. Denise wasn't sure she wanted to see what kind of horrible person was shacking up in the room next door, and wondered if violence would ensue. At the same time, going back to her room or waiting downstairs didn't sound like great options either.

"I'll come with you. Don't you think you should take something as a precaution? Like a weapon, in case there's someone squatting in the room? Like a homeless person?"

Bonnie chuckled, "Oh, I don't think that's necessary. We've never had a break-in, and if someone was in there, I would've seen them or heard the bell jangle when they came in. They couldn't get in through the window. There's no way to access that room other than from coming in the front door. All our windows are locked from the inside. Let's just go see what's going on."

When the innkeeper came around the desk, Denise noticed that she had bare feet, but didn't want to draw any attention to it since she felt it might be rude to mention. So she followed the elderly woman up the stairs and onto the second floor hallway. As they walked, neither of them said anything, but Bonnie had begun whistling a strange tune that Denise had never heard before.

Once in front of the door outside of Room Eight, Denise felt the tension begin to curl underneath her shoulder blades.

"Be careful," she advised.

Bonnie didn't respond and simply reached out and unlocked the door with a key that also contained the strange insignia. Denise held her breath as the door slowly opened and the two peered inside.

The room was empty and terribly bare. Compared to the room she shared with Lilly, Denise was shocked to see the sparseness of the room.

A single bed was in the center of the room and was covered by a plain white sheet. Two thin pillows rested atop the bedding. The floor was worn and a television that looked like it was an antique was positioned atop a bare table. There was no entertainment center, no desk, and the walls were bare. The window was a single-pane structure and when Bonnie jiggled it, it didn't move.

A cursory view of the bathroom didn't reveal anything either. Just a tiny shower and a toilet that looked like it hadn't been cleaned in months. The smell of mildew hung in the air, and Denise realized that she urgently wanted to get out of the room as quickly as possible.

"See? There's nobody here. This is one of our older rooms that we plan on renovating."

Bonnie walked out of the room and waited for Denise to exit, before she turned around and locked the door behind them. The two women stood face-to-face for a moment before Denise spoke.

"I don't understand. There was somebody in there. I swear to you, I heard someone curse at me when I was standing on the other side of the doorway."

Bonnie sighed as if she was irritated and was ready to put the whole situation to rest. "I'm sorry, Ms. Paskins, but there is no one there. Not sure what else I can do to help. Maybe it's time to call it a night?"

Normally, Denise would've been irritated at the suggestion as it was not Bonnie's place to tell her when to call it a night. She was an adult after all. However, given the circumstances, she simply dropped her head and nodded, feeling embarrassed about the whole situation.

As Bonnie began to walk away, Denise remembered the symbols on the desk.

"Bonnie?"

The woman stopped walking and turned around slowly. For a split second, Denise thought the woman looked furious, almost murderous, but the look disappeared and was replaced by a smile.

"Yes?"

"Sorry to bring this up, and it may not be anything. I'm curious, though. When I went to your desk, I noticed that you had some papers with these strange symbols written on it. What was that?"

Bonnie looked at her for a moment and then spoke softly, "Oh, that was just some material I was working on. It's nothing to worry about. Just some nonsense from an old woman who has too much time on her hands." And with that, she chuckled again, turned and went downstairs.

Denise stood in the hallway for a moment, and tried to calm her nerves. Bonnie's abrupt departure had left her feeling uneasy and ridiculous.

The room was empty. So that means that the sounds were coming from someplace else. But from where, exactly? Or maybe there's someone in the hotel trying to play pranks on us?

Exhaustion began peeling away her resolve, and Denise decided that the best thing to do was to get some sleep and find another hotel in the morning.

I'm sure we can find something with the help of GPS. I'll just start driving north. Since the hurricane is supposed to hit Miami around midnight, some people may be trying to drive back as soon as it's over. Not sure how smart that is, but at least it will leave some vacancies for those of us who are waiting a few more days before returning. Lilly's school is closed for the rest of the week so we should be fine.

Removing the key from her pocket, Denise inserted it into the lock on her door and turned it, feeling a burst of relief when she heard the telltale click. The knob turned easily in her hand.

She pushed the door open and closed it quickly behind her,

locking it again and sighing loudly.

"So, what happened?" Lilly asked. She was lying on the bed and watching a sitcom, with the volume turned down very low.

"Nothing. There was no one there." Denise didn't feel like elaborating because she was too tired.

"What do you mean there was no one there? Mom, I'm telling you the truth. I heard someone in there. There were all these strange sounds coming from that room. I'm not making it up. Honest."

"I know. I trust you. But I think we should probably just go to bed. There's nothing else we can do tonight."

Lilly looked unconvinced. She gave her mother a large pout and then twirled around, storming off to the room with the other bed.

Denise considered following after her, but just couldn't muster up the energy. She fell forward, fully clothed, and closed her eyes the minute her head hit the pillow.

4

The sound of wind rattling the window frames, woke Lilly out of a deep sleep. She could hear the sounds and struggled to keep her eyes shut but her young mind had already started pulling her into consciousness.

Lilly

She heard a woman whisper her name.

Lilly

Lilly opened her eyes and looked around. The room was dark and small, consisting of a bed and a small dresser. The door to the remainder of the room was open and beyond, nothing but black.

She couldn't remember if she had shut the door on not. But now, it was open and she had no choice but to go back to sleep or shut it.

Someone called out my name.

Lilly felt a chill go down her spine. She knew that it was best to remain in place, lying in bed and just wait for morning. But something was pulling her out of bed, gently guiding her across the floor, and leading her to the window that overlooked the back of the hotel.

Outside, the world was dark and wet. Raindrops splattered against the glass, and the trees lining the perimeter of the hotel swayed to and fro in an insane dance only possible due to the ferocity of Mother Nature.

Suddenly, Lilly saw a black figure standing on the ground near the trees. At first, she thought it might be her imagination, and given what she'd heard next door only to find out that no one was there—made her wonder if she could trust any of her senses … however, the figure went from a solid black to having a shape and a face.

There's a woman down there! What is she doing outside in the rain?

A feeling of warmth started in Lilly's feet and slowly spread along her legs, traveling up her body. It was an uncomfortable sensation and for a brief moment she worried that she had wet her pants. It spread up her neck and then along her head, permeating her mind with a foggy heat that shut out all reason.

Come to me, Lilly.

She could feel her body turn and her legs start to move. She was no longer in control of herself, and it felt like something was pulling her forward with invisible strings. The analogy of a remote control car or a puppet popped into her mind and she felt scared—wanting to scream. But something was keeping all of her emotions bottled inside, and the unexpressed panic dissipated into a painful, fearful sensation.

Lilly turned and moved away from the window, exiting her room. She walked into the main area of the hotel room where she could see her mother sleeping on the bed. A tear leaked out of the corner of her eye because she wanted to turn her head and shout out, but she was unable to.

Lilly opened the door, easily turning the knob with a wrist that no longer felt her own. She hoped that her mother would see the sliver of light enter from the hallway, but to her horror—the hallway was now dark as night.

Oh, no. I don't want to go there. It looks scary. No. Please no. Mom, wake up! Wake up!

Her bare feet proceeded forward and the door to the hotel room remained open behind her. As she traveled down the hallway, Lilly could feel the soft carpet underneath her toes. Her body continued forward and began to descend the stairwell.

The stairwell was still lit by the strange candles, only now ... they were real. Small embers flickered from the flames that gently swayed to and fro. Lilly could see wax dripping down the white sticks onto metal platforms that were shaped in the same insignia as the key to their room.

When she reached the bottom floor, her body turned expertly and maneuvered itself past the lounge and then, past the front desk, which was empty. Lilly had hoped that maybe Bonnie was nearby, but the woman was nowhere to be found.

Her arm extended, a hand reaching for the front door.

And then...

... she was outside in the dark with the rain and wind.

5

1:00 AM

The urge to urinate was non-stop and irritating.

Denise tried to ignore it for about ten minutes, but the sensation was keeping her up, so she rose and stumbled to the bathroom door. When she flicked on the light inside the bathroom, she realized that she'd made the entire motion with her eyes closed, and now with the harsh fluorescent light shining down on her—she took a brief look in the mirror.

Whoa. I look pretty rough. This interesting evening has definitely taken its toll on me.

After a quick stint on the toilet, Denise arose and leaned forward to wash her hands in the sink.

When she looked in the mirror again, she saw a dark shape standing behind her.

What the fuck?

Denise turned around quickly, her heart nearly jumping out its cavity.

There was no one there. She was alone in the bathroom.

"Wow," she whispered to herself. "I'm seeing things now. Wonderful."

When she turned back to the sink, she saw a piece of red hair in the basin. It was curly and long, and undoubtedly had been attached to her daughter's head at one time. Finding long red hairs when Lilly was around (and even when she wasn't at home) wasn't an unusual occurrence.

Denise smiled and turned on the water, watching the strand of hair go round and round until it dropped into the drain and disappeared.

She looked around one more time to ensure she was alone in the bathroom and satisfied that there was no one there, walked out and shut the door quietly behind her.

Maybe I should check on Lilly. Just want to be sure she is ok. We left things on kind of a tense note.

Denise noticed that the door to Lilly's room was cracked open, and she figured that her daughter had come out to use the bathroom sometime earlier, which would explain the obvious evidence in the sink.

Denise pushed lightly on the door and struggled to see inside. She could see a lumpy mass on Lilly's bed, and was about to turn around and go back to sleep—not wanting to wake up her daughter, when something stopped her.

The room felt entirely too still.

The air was stagnant and even the wind outside seemed to have calmed down. Denise knew that her daughter wasn't a heavy sleeper and tended to thrash around, so the quiet was odd.

She moved toward the bed and reached out to gently pull back the blanket.

When she did, what she found was a mass of pine cones, dirt and strangely knotted twine.

Oh my God. What is this?

Not even taking a breath, Denise ran to the wall and flipped on the lights. The room filled with an artificial glow and it was immediately clear that her daughter was gone. Panic bubbled up in her chest and the room started to spin around her.

Got to stay calm. She probably just wandered into the hallway again. I'm sure once I head out there, she'll be standing in front of the room next door again. Just need to take deep breaths. One at a time.

Denise gritted her teeth together and walked back into the main room. It was then that she noticed the door to their room was open. Beyond that, she couldn't see much.

Fear building up in her body, Denise slipped on a pair of flip flops and arranged her pajama pants so that she looked presentable. She moved slowly into the open hallway and noticed that all the lights were out except for the EXIT sign above the stairwell. Still, it was enough to give her a visual so that she was able to walk around without bumping into walls.

The hallway was empty, but the door to Room Eight was ajar.

Taking a deep breath, Denise began walking toward it. Horrible visions filled her mind, and she struggled to maintain control. She didn't want to imagine what horrors could befall her ten-year-old daughter in a hotel that was slowly turning into a horror show.

This may all be a big mistake. Why can't this all be a big mistake? What if Lilly has been hurt? I'll kill anyone who hurts my precious girl. She's only ten! What would anyone want with her? She is too young to bother anyone! What if she is sleepwalking and angered some crazy guy next door? She's never sleepwalked before.

There was no light coming from Room Eight, so Denise reached around the doorframe, trying to feel around for a switch. She moved her hand blindly around the wall until she felt a smooth plastic lever and quickly pressed on it.

Yellow-orange light seemed to burst into the darkness, and somewhere within the room glass cracked and broke. Denise figured a bulb had burst and stepped into the room to take a closer look.

The room looked similar to the way it had appeared when she'd visited it hours before with Bonnie. Only now, the bed looked larger and didn't seem to be in exactly the same spot as before. It also had a large pile of dirt, pine cones and twigs on it, neatly arranged in a pile at the center of the mattress.

"Lilly!" Denise called out, her voice wavering from fear. "Lilly, are you in here?"

The only reply was the howl of the wind as it shook the windows.

Not willing to hesitate a moment more, Denise reached for her cell phone. Without a moment's consideration, she dialed 9-1-1.

She listened to a ringing sound, and then...

"Jackson County Sheriff's Department."

"I need your help, immediately."

A pause and then, a concerned voice with a strong Southern drawl asked, "Yes, ma'am. What seems to be the problem?"

"My daughter, she's missing. We're staying at the Countryside Inn and somehow, I've lost her. I don't know where she is, and it's so dark and windy outside. Please come quickly. My name is Denise Paskins and her name is Lilly

Paskins. She's only ten. The Inn. Please help!"

Another pause and then, "Where did you say you were staying"

Denise was losing her patience, "We are at the Countryside Inn. Please, I need help. Fast!"

Again, the operator on the other line paused and then spoke slowly, "I understand, and don't worry. We'll find her. This weather isn't helping, that's for sure. We're getting so many calls from frantic folks. The power's out in many places too. Don't worry. I'll send someone out to you immediately."

"Thank you, thank you." Denise hung up the phone, and wrung her hands—feeling a bit better.

She looked around the room once more, and began wandering around, searching for clues to where her daughter had gone. But other than the mess on the bed, there was nothing else out of place.

That's the second time I've seen all that kind of stuff on a bed. First on Lilly's and now in here. That's not a coincidence. I've got to find Lilly. Something horrible is happening here. Something not normal.

Just then, Denise heard the sound of a door banging. It sounded like the front of the hotel.

Lilly! She may be down there!

Racing from the room, Denise didn't bother to put on slippers or change into clean clothes. She ran down the hallway and then down the stairs, barely taking a breath as she moved as quickly as she could.

The downstairs lobby was dark. The front desk, empty.

"Hello? Is anyone down here? Bonnie, are you here?"

When no one answered, Denise went behind the counter and found the light switch, flicking it on quickly. Unlike the rooms upstairs, the downstairs seemed to be without power and it was difficult to see. A full moon hung in the cloudy skies outside and periodically offered its glow to help her. Other than that, she was relying on memory to find her way.

She felt around the desk and was surprised that there wasn't much stored there. A few stray pieces of paper, impossible to read in the darkness, fluttered to the floor as she reached around, trying to find a flashlight. Then, an idea struck her.

The candles! There were candles in the stairwell, and they looked real. I can grab one of those!

After a few stumbles, Denise found her way back to the stairwell. Real candles now lined the ascending alcove and she reached out carefully, grasping a metal holder that contained a candle that hadn't burned too far down.

Denise returned to the front desk and continued to look around to no avail. It was strangely bare.

Time to check Bonnie's room. That lady was all friendly when we got here but she didn't seem all that understanding when checking on Room Eight. And what about all that writing I found?

Denise picked up the papers and tried to read them by candlelight. To her surprise, each sheet was blank. She picked up page after page and the result was the same. A blank page, with no writing it, no lines, nothing scribbled … nothing.

After trying to find anything of substance, Denise turned and began walking down a short hallway that she presumed led to the innkeeper's quarters. She walked a few feet and saw a door at the end of the hallway. It was closed.

"Bonnie? Are you in there? I don't want to wake you but my daughter' missing, and I need your help."

Denise strained to hear a response, and in the distance she thought she heard a woman laugh. It was faint and menacing— and nothing like the woman she had met earlier.

"Bonnie?" She tried again. "Is that you? I really need to talk to you."

Silence.

Reaching out, Denise tried the knob. The door wasn't locked and the knob turned in her hand. Pushing the door open, Denise was sure to keep the candle in front of her so that she could see her surroundings. The room looked sparse and it was empty, but a slew of papers stuck to the wall drew her attention.

The papers had rudimentary and simple drawings on them. One had an image of what looked like a wolf's head. The other one had scratchy drawings of trees on it. A third had a red circle drawn in the center of it, and a fourth had symbols written on it.

The same symbols Denise had seen on the paper at the front desk.

She searched around for nearly ten minutes, frantically trying to find anything that made sense, when a voice called out from behind her.

"Hello? Is anyone here?"

A man that looked to be in his twenties, in uniform and carrying a bright flashlight shone it right into Denise's face, momentarily blinding her.

"Ma'am, is everything here ok?"

Denise tried to keep her temper under control. "No, everything is not ok, and would you mind moving that flashlight somewhere else?"

"Oh, so sorry. Are you the person who called us earlier?"

"Yes, I'm Denise Paskins. My daughter, Lilly. She's missing. I need your help to find her. I've tried to find her and there's no one here at the hotel. I can't even find the innkeeper, Bonnie. And now the power is out down here."

The deputy looked confused for a minute, and then rubbed his head before answering.

"I'm sorry Ms. Paskins, but the reason this building is empty and the power's not working is because ... well, this inn's been closed for about five years. The owners come back every so often from Alabama to check in on it, and I think there is a groundskeeper, but other than that—it's pretty much closed for business."

Shit. What the hell is going on here?

Denise tried to calm down so that she could speak without getting hysterical. "Ok, I understand what you're saying but there was a woman here. Her name was Bonnie and she checked us into the inn. She didn't say anything about this place being closed or anything like that. Why would she do that?"

"I don't know what to tell you. I've never heard of a woman named Bonnie working here. The groundskeeper is a man named Harold, and like I said—he doesn't come here all that often. I think someone's trying to take you for a ride. But don't worry. We'll find your daughter. She couldn't have gotten very far. These woods are pretty dense, and it isn't easy to get around in them."

Suddenly, the wind howled and shook the windows fiercely.

Denise pulled on her sleeves and wrapped her arms around her body. She couldn't seem to focus and wondered if this was what going into shock was like.

"This weather isn't going to help us," the deputy continued, "but I've got another flashlight and a jacket in my car. If you want, I can grab it for you."

Denise nodded. She couldn't seem to get the words out, and her mouth felt dry.

"Ok, I'll go grab everything. By the way, my name's Rodriguez. You can just call me Rod for short."

When Denise remained silent, Rod simply nodded and went outside to get the flashlight and the jacket, leaving Denise in the darkness once more.

She shivered and looked around. Everything seemed more ominous now, and even the darkness seemed … *blacker.*

This makes no sense. I feel like I'm trapped in a nightmare and can't wake up. Why would Bonnie have made all that effort to pretend like this was a legitimate inn, only to kidnap Lilly? What if she is going to do something strange to my daughter? And all those crazy symbols? We need to find Lilly as soon as possible. And then I need to get as far away from here as I can.

Just then, a woman started laughing upstairs. The sound echoed throughout the building and was enough to send Denise racing for the door.

"Well, there doesn't seem to be anyone up here. Are you sure you heard a woman? I've checked the hallways and each room with those weird keys, and each one is empty."

Denise shook her head. "There was someone laughing up here. I swear to you. But you know, I've been hearing weird things all night, and the place is empty. Honestly, can we just get out of here and start looking for Lilly? I don't want to waste another minute."

Rod sighed. "It's not going to be easy. You need to stay close to my side and if you hear or see anything, let me be the one to deal with it. Understood?"

"Understood."

6

2:30 AM

The sky was dark, and the winds were warm—tropical storm-type gusts that carried rain with the same hot temperatures. On the other side of the road, the trees whipped back and forth, thrust in different directions by storm bands that had somehow made their way to the depths of Georgia.

Rod took a cursory look around and decided that it would be best for them to begin searching the back of the inn first.

Whatever that kid was thinking, she wouldn't have just run across the street into that shit over there. I don't care how angry she was at her mom or what she was running toward—she wouldn't have gone into the woods on the other side of the street. That's scary stuff—even for grown adults. And if she did, then we're going to need more people to help out than just me and her mother.

Rod had serious doubts about Denise. She was completely disheveled and had told him that she'd checked into an inn that had obviously been closed for a while. He wasn't sure if she was telling him the truth, but if her daughter really was missing—if she even had a daughter—he couldn't imagine an abduction having taken place. The roads were relatively quiet because of the storm, which last he heard was moving much more quickly than anticipated and was already impacting Georgia. Protocol was that he couldn't put out any alerts until the child had been missing for at least 12 hours. So, while he wanted to help the obviously distressed woman, he was aware that the whole effort might be a huge waste of time.

"And you're sure she wasn't angry with you?" he asked for the second time.

"No. She wasn't angry. This is completely unlike her. Something is wrong," Denise insisted.

Rod nodded. "Ok, if that's the case, let's check the back of the hotel first to see if maybe we can find her. Stay close to me. It's dark, and I don't want you to slip and fall on anything."

Together, they walked slowly around the inn to the back yard. As they passed the side of the hotel, Rod took a cursory look over his left shoulder. The inn was starting to fall into disrepair. Vines snaked up along the walls and had begun to wrap themselves around the window panes. Some of the windows were cracked and moss was growing under some of the panels.

For a moment he thought he saw a light in one of the windows, but then it disappeared and he wondered if the moon had managed to shine a bit of light, causing the reflective phenomenon.

They continued until they reached the back of the hotel, which consisted of a large courtyard with a dried-up fountain in the center, now filled with rain water. A deranged looking cherub child held a pot and kept it a slanted angle, which would have allowed water to flow back into the base of the fountain.

Rod thought it was hideous.

Behind the fountain, a wall of trees swayed back and forth.

"Ok, she's obviously not out here. Let's check behind those trees. Lilly! Are you over here?"

Rod shined his flashlight over the trees and wet leaves shone in the brightness of the light. He moved the beam back and forth.

"Lilly! Are you out here?"

They both called for Lilly as the two moved closer to the trees and then past them into the darkness of the woods.

"Be careful," Rod instructed. "There's a creek back here that runs the span of these grounds. Keep an eye out for it. You don't want to fall in by accident."

Denise nodded and kept close, her eyes wide.

Rod continued to shine his flashlight from left to right, doing his best to light up the perimeter.

"Lilly! Where are you?"

7

When Lilly finally regained control of her body, she crumpled to the ground in exhaustion. She barely felt the branches or stones underneath her knees—the relief of having control back overpowered everything.

She had no idea where she was. Her body had taken her away from the hotel and deep into the woods. It felt like she'd been walking for hours, unable to stop. And now, she was in the middle of ... well, she had no idea where.

Lilly wanted to shout for help, but her throat was dry, and she was frightened of making a sound. She knew that whatever had taken control of her legs wasn't far away.

If I scream, whatever it is will hear me. But I don't want to be stuck here. I want my mom. We need to get away from here—this place is bad. I'm just going to have to find my way back.

Walking wasn't easy. With bare feet, Lilly felt stabbing pain each time she took a step forward. And she wasn't entirely sure which direction to move in. The trees around her looked identical in the dark. Everything was tall and wet, branches sticking out in wayward directions.

At times, she thought there was a light in the distance, but it was simply the moon reflecting off the droplets of water that clung to each branch.

Lilly knew that she was in danger, but wasn't entirely panicked. In her young mind, there was still an area that simply wouldn't accept that anything bad could happen. So she pressed on, pushing her feet forward as the woods continued to wrap her in misshapen, bent arms.

The air, which had smelled dank—was now taking on a different aroma. It started to smell like a fire was burning nearby.

Lilly stopped and sniffed.

It smells like when Mom is barbequing at the park. Not just like fire, but also like meat cooking. If there's meat, then there has to be people too. I just need to keep walking. These woods won't go on forever.

Suddenly, Lilly saw flickering light in the distance. It was low to the ground and reddish-yellow. She had a difficult time making out anything else, but felt her heart rate increase.

There are people out there. Not sure if they are good or bad. Need to go slowly and make sure everything is ok before I say anything.

She crept along, trying to be as quiet as possible as the rains overhead began pelting her with a ferocity reserved for tropical storm bands.

Denise heard the creek before they came upon it. Despite the rain now falling in sheets around them, she could also hear a different sound—water rushing in one direction.

Rod had given her an umbrella but even with protection from the wind, it was difficult to communicate because of the constant howling of the storm. She was also getting wet because at times, the wind carried the falling rain in a vertical position, hitting her from underneath the umbrella.

"Rod!" she shouted, "I see the creek! Should we check there?"

He didn't answer and instead, pointed his flashlight toward the rushing water. "Lilly! Are you out here?"

They both stood together and waited for several minutes, calling out periodically for the missing girl.

After a moment, Denise shouted again, "She's not out here! We need to check on the other side of the road! We're wasting valuable time!"

Rod stared out toward the creek, his frustration apparent as he shook his head, wiping his face in concern.

"Alright. But first, I'm going to call the station for backup. This weather's getting worse and we'll need some reinforcement if we're going to head into those woods."

We're wasting time. We need to find her.

Denise bit back tears as she followed Rod back to his patrol car.

Claire Delaney was tired of the constant rain. She was off the clock in less than one hour, and wasn't looking forward to navigating her small four-door compact car along the winding roads that led to her parents' house. They lived in the Fox

Trace community that was located off the Veterans Memorial Parkway. There were very few lights along the winding roads that traveled up and down numerous hills. More than once she had nearly swerved off the road to avoid a truck that was entirely too large to be traveling along that stretch of highway.

At twenty-two, Claire knew she was too old to be living with her parents. She had opted for work after high school instead of going away to college, and the result was landing a job as a communications operator at the Sherriff's satellite station. She knew that it was a good job, and she took it seriously. But at times it could be isolating, and on a night when a storm was blowing through—there were other places she wanted to be.

Like home in my bed.

The station was quiet, with very few deputies calling in. There were seven on duty, and for the most part, they were driving around in the rain, keeping an eye on the power outages and trying to keep the locals from getting into too much trouble. Claire was also keeping an eye on the local news and from what the anchors were saying, approximately 300,000 people in Georgia from Atlanta northward were without power. It was strange because the hurricane was hammering South Florida, but somehow, a secondary storm had formed ahead of the hurricane and was traveling due north.

And now, some crazy lady was saying that her daughter had been abducted from the Countryside Inn.

That place has been closed for like … forever. Another nut job.

The lights flickered, and Claire looked around nervously. She was the only one physically at the station and if the lights went out, she was fearful that the generator might not kick on.

Relax. You are freaking yourself out.

"Unit Six to base. Unit Six to base."

Oh, thank goodness. Rod. Finally, someone is actually reaching out to me.

"This is base. What's your ETA, Unit Six?"

Rod sounded breathless and frustrated.

"ETA is undetermined. Requesting back-up. We've got a missing girl out by the old inn on Route 46. I think this may be legit. The weather is starting to get bad out here. Gonna need some help."

Claire ran the numbers in her head. Deputy Cantra was closest. Deputy McPherson was about ten minutes south of them.

I'll send both. If there's a child somewhere out in this mess, Rod's going to need as much help as he can get.

"Unit Six, I'm sending Cantra and McPherson. 10-4."

"Got it. Thanks. Over and out."

Claire took a deep breath and rubbed her eyes.

This is going to be a long night.

8

The burnt smell of fire and animal fat grew stronger as Lilly neared the flickering lights. As she peeked around the trees, she could see that the glow was indeed part of a mid-sized fire originating from a fire pit that was controlled by a series of large stones in a semi-circle.

There were people sitting around the fire—all women.

The women had long hair, and were wearing loose-fitting dark garments. They sat together, speaking quietly and every so often, one of them pushed a stick into the fire to kindle the flames. Despite the heavier rains, the fire burned bright and Lilly was able to feel warmth even from her hidden vantage point.

She was unsure what to do, but figured that a group of women sitting around a fireplace weren't all that dangerous.

They look kinda old. And none of them have guns or anything. How dangerous can they be? Also, I am getting wet, and I'm scared. Maybe they are just camping and can help me find my way out. They are kind of creepy, but I don't have any other choice. Maybe they have little girls like me too.

Lilly moved slowly and stepped on a twig. The snap wasn't all that loud, but she jumped from surprise.

At that moment, and without turning around, one of the women spoke.

"Come out of the darkness, child. You must be freezing. Why don't you sit here by the fire with us?"

"You see me?" Lilly asked, dumbfounded.

"We see everything. No need to hide in the rain. Come out here and sit with us by the fire."

The women chuckled amongst themselves. Their voices were old and scratchy, but not frightening. They all remained in a seated position and none of them looked over at Lilly.

"Well, I guess I probably should," Lilly said hesitantly.

The women chuckled again, and one of them shifted over to make room.

Feeling shy amongst the group, Lilly kept her head down and sat on a log next to the woman who was closest to her.

"That's good. See? It's not raining over here."

To her surprise, Lilly felt the rain stop almost immediately. Instead, she felt the warmth from the fire encircle her face and legs. It was a welcome respite from the wind and rain, but she wasn't entirely comfortable.

Rain doesn't just stop falling. There is something about these women. Something about this fire. Why do I feel so sleepy all of a sudden?

Lilly felt her eyes drawn to the fire. It was a magnetic sight, flames leaping up toward the sky and the constant crackling of the wood. She wanted to ask questions, wanted to get help from the strange group but found that her mouth wasn't working anymore.

She felt hazy suddenly, drunk on an invisible port that smelled and tasted like burnt air.

Her eyes beginning to droop, Lilly turned her head to look at the woman next to her.

A mop of frizzy hair framed the face of a hag that was wizened to the point of agelessness. She had small beady eyes and a very large nose that curved downward.

Lilly was reminded of a witch in countless fairy tales. She stared into the small eyes, fully aware that her own vision was quickly failing.

Unable to speak, she simply stared until the darkness swept in and her body began to collapse.

"That's right," the woman said. "Let it happen. Just let it happen. That's a good girl."

The Elder was pleased. The approaching storm signaled that the time of initiation was fast approaching. The continuation of the coven needed to be preserved, and there had been loss throughout the decade. Some had left of their own free will, others had joined the creator, and there was one who existed on her own—serving as a scout for the group. She was mysterious and powerful, sometimes veering from teachings that had helped her get to a position of autonomy.

This witch, also known to the group as Sephira, did not hide her fondness for black magic, and the Elder knew that this was a dangerous practice. Black magic brought with it a level of darkness and activated evil spirits that were drawn to such activities.

Sephira had contaminated several areas of the state with her spells, including the inn where the young girl and her mother were staying. The elder herself was fearful of that place. It was worse than simply abandoned ... it was dark and filled with creatures conjured from Sephira's spells.

The coven practiced conscious cooperation. They did not want witches to join them under the threat of fear of death. But children had to be handled differently. When a child entered their realm, whether by encouragement or by curiosity, certain measures had to be taken to ensure compliance.

She looked over at the child lying on the ground.

They'd been watching Lilly for a while. Her birth during the full moon had been marked by the creator. She was easy to connect with and luring her out to join them had been easy. It wasn't always easy. They'd lost most of their sisters.

But this one was different.

The Elder looked around her and felt a wave of sadness. The other women were worn out and even the spells of revitalization weren't helping anymore. There was a weariness she saw in the eyes of those closest to her. At times they would cast an illusion and once again look youthful, the fruits of magic covering them in a soft, innocent light. But for many of them, the ability to use magic was becoming more difficult, and with each passing year—it grew worse.

We must find a way to extend the bloodline. If we don't, then our entire coven will cease to exist. Just a few powerful ones are all we need. And then we can rest.

A hand suddenly rested on her shoulder. The Elder didn't have to turn around to know that it was the youngest of the group, Nyssa who was now standing behind her.

"What is it?" She asked without turning around.

"We should make haste. There are others looking for her. She won't stay this way for long."

The Elder nodded. "Let's carry her back to the inn. The spells should hold so that we have enough time and privacy to complete the ritual. If anyone should bother us, there are many things we can do to prevent additional delay."

With the assistance of the other witches, the women lifted Lilly and slowly carried her back through the woods.

9

Deputy Javier Cantra wasn't having a good night. In fact, there were so many things going wrong lately that it was hard for him to focus on one particular issue.

He hated living in Georgia, for starters. A Miami boy at heart, he'd moved to North Georgia to start over after his marriage to Sharon had ended. She'd been a spitfire from the very start, and his parents had warned him that a *Gringa* would only bring him trouble. And she had. Spent nearly every cent they had earned during their 5-year marriage on a secret gambling addiction. Left him with nothing but the clothes in his closet and a meager 401k savings account that he'd opened during his short time with the Miami-Dade police department.

Thankfully, they hadn't brought any kids into their contaminated marriage, but the years of loss and heartache had done him in. He now harbored a very private bout with alcoholism and his confidence had taken a beating. Despite being a relatively handsome guy, he avoided dating and when he wasn't working, he spent most of his time at home with a can of beer in his hand—trying to forget the past.

Working during an oncoming storm didn't bother him necessarily, but his headache from a hangover wasn't helping matters. He'd been drinking too much lately, and the time it took to recover was getting longer and longer.

Or I'm just drinking more and more.

Javier rubbed his face and squinted, trying to maintain his position on the road. He'd always had difficulty with night vision, and the roads leading up to the inn weren't exactly lit brightly.

Damn hillbillies. I need to find another place to live. This just isn't working for me.

Suddenly, something raced across the road in front of him. Javier slammed on the brakes and for an instant, saw a woman who looked about three-hundred-years-old standing in the middle of the road. Her eyes were entirely black and her mouth was opened widely.

Shit!

The tires couldn't find any traction and he felt the vehicle begin to spin. Trying to ease up on the gas, Javier tried to steady the wheel and held his breath as the car veered off the road and stopped in an embankment on the side of the road. The front of the car was pointed down and the back tires were slightly off the ground.

Uninjured, he removed his seatbelt and carefully opened the driver's side door, letting his body drop to the ground. It wasn't a far drop, but as soon as his body left the car, the vehicle slid further forward and was now resting at an alarming angle. It was pointing down toward the embankment.

One thing was crystal clear—there was no way to push the car out of its current situation without some towing support. It was also drizzling, and Javier wondered how long it would take for the rains to come down ferociously. He'd seen the weather report. The longer he stayed out in the dark, the harder the rains would be. Not a very good combination.

"Unit Five. Unit Five, do you copy? This is base. Checking status. What's your estimated ETA?"

Javier shook his head. There was no way he could radio back, so he reached for his cell phone and was thankful when his hand touched the cool smoothness of the screen. He dialed quickly and took a deep breath, determined not to sound shaken from the accident.

The phone rang twice and then Claire answered. She sounded tired.

"Jackson County Sheriff's Department. How can I help you?"

"Claire, it's Javier. I've had an accident."

A pause on the other line, and then, "An accident? Oh my God. Are you ok? Where are you?"

Javier looked ahead and could see the inn, just a little further down the road. "Real close to the inn. Less than a mile north off of Route 46. Something ran out in front of me, and I lost control of my vehicle. The roads are real slick out here right now." Javier stopped, unsure of what else to say. He also remembered what had caused him to career off the road in the first place and wondered what it was that he'd seen.

"You're going to need towing?" Claire asked, breaking his train of thought.

"Yeah. I can leave the car here for now and just walk over. Should only take me a few minutes. You going to be ok to send someone over?"

"Yeah, no problem. You can just ride back with Rodriguez. When you get over there, just have him radio me so I know everything's ok."

Javier looked around. It was very quiet and he assumed the squad car up ahead at the inn wasn't running because the darkness was complete—no sounds of an engine running or beaming headlights.

"Ok, no problem. Thanks, Claire."

Hanging up the phone, he placed it back in his pocket and walked back over to the car. The force of the accident had knocked his flashlight into the passenger seat, so he carefully reached over and retrieved it—trying not to apply any additional pressure to the vehicle.

"Ok," he said aloud to himself, "Let's go."

Acutely aware that he may not be alone, Javier shined his flashlight along the sides of the road looking to see if any strange old woman was hobbling near the trees. Instead, he scared a few squirrels and a deer that was seeking refuge from the oncoming storm.

He continued walking along the road until he arrived at the inn. At first glance, the building looked as deserted as always, the windows reflecting the moonlight and not much else. But then, he though he saw an orange light flickering near one of the upstairs windows.

Oh shit. I hope the place hasn't caught fire or something. That could be a huge mess. I'd better go check it out, and then I'll come back outside and radio Rodriguez so I can help him look for this missing girl.

Javier walked up to the squad car and looked inside. The driver's door wasn't locked so he assumed Rod was somewhere in the general vicinity.

Or maybe he's inside there. Maybe he needs my help.

Subconsciously, Javier reached down and felt his gun resting in its holster. He took a deep breath and opened the front door.

The door swung open and he was met by a musty-humid smell that was common in old, unused buildings. Rubbing his nose, he stepped inside and used his flashlight to look around.

The front desk looked dusty and unused with a few ancillary papers lying on the desk that were unreadable in the darkness. To his left, he saw some chairs, a sofa and a coffee table that were unimpressive and had clearly been left behind to rot.

Thump

The noise came from somewhere upstairs and caught Javier off guard. He felt his bladder loosen from the surprise, and tugged on his penis to offset the sudden need to urinate.

This is ridiculous. I shouldn't be such a pussy. There's probably nothing up there.

"Hello?" he called out, hoping that Rod was up there.

When no one answered, he took another deep breath and wiped his forehead. He was feeling very warm and dizzy— wanting to get the upstairs search over with as quickly as possible.

"Ok, I'm coming up," he said in a shaky voice.

The stairwell was very narrow and he noticed the strange candles that ran along the wall. Nothing was lit however, and he wondered where the orange light had come from or if the entire thing had simply been his imagination.

Maybe I'm just drinking too much. I could've imagined it. There's nothing here. It's just a shitty rundown hotel. That's all.

Upstairs, Javier could barely breathe. It was stifling. The air was stagnant, musky and full of dust. He stifled a sneeze and rubbed his nose again, trying to pull it together. He felt strange and disconnected, the darkness feeling like arms that were squeezing the air out of his lungs.

"Hello?" Javier called out again, this time softer than before.

Nothing at first, and then … he smelled something very familiar.

The smell of a bar hit him with such familiarity that at first he thought he was back at *Jerry's Wet Whistle*, a local bar where he spent most of his time staring into a half-empty glass. He could almost see the yellow-brown liquid pooling at the bottom of his tumbler, just waiting for that final sip.

Feeling his mouth water, Javier tried to reconcile the feelings crowding him. He knew that it was completely irrational to be smelling the scents of a local bar while he was standing in the middle of a deserted inn. But at the same time, he was almost *glad* and wondered how bad it would really be if he just happened to find a room full of liquor or beer. Or both.

The idea was strangely exciting.

Javier wasn't entirely sure where the smell was coming from, so he started checking each room, one by one. It was easy to do because all the doors were slightly ajar, making the rooms immediately accessible.

In one of the rooms, he saw Denise's suitcase and the mussed beds. But there was no one there. He wondered what would have led the woman to think that the inn was inhabitable.

Maybe she's a nutcase. How could someone bring her young daughter into a place like this? I know there's a storm coming but there's plenty of normal places in town. This makes no sense. I hope Rod knows what he's getting into. It's quite possible that this woman did something to her kid and she's trying to make it look like an accident.

It was time to check the final room in the hallway. Thus far, he'd found nothing.

The last room on the right was farther away from the other doors, and Javier figured that at one time it had served as a suite.

He pushed on the door.

"Hello? Is anyone in there?"

A dull blue light spilled out into the hallway as the door swung open further.

Javier pulled his gun from the holster, removed the safety and put his finger on the trigger, ready to shoot if needed. Kicking the door fully open, he peered around the corner and his eyes widened at the sight.

The room wasn't a room at all. It was a bar, fully stocked. At one end, rows of mirrored shelving lined the wall, filled with bottles full of liquid that Javier recognized from his many trips to local watering holes.

Forgetting his need to urinate, Javier's lips itched with the desire to quench a deep-seated thirst that was getting worse and worse. The fire in his belly burned with an aching to feel the numbness that accompanied each swallow of alcohol.

The fact that a bar had appeared in the middle of a long-closed inn was troubling, but Javier felt any concern strangely melt away as he neared the oak surface of the bar top. To his delight, a bottle of Jack Daniels sat near the ledge, with a sparkling tumbler right next to it.

Without taking even the slightest moment to consider what was unfolding around him, Javier stepped up to the bar, put the gun back into the holster and then tightly grasped the bottle with his hand. With an expert fluidity reserved for heavier drinkers in need of satiating, he removed the cap from the bottle and poured the amber liquid into the nearby tumbler.

Within moments, he had tipped the glass back and was pouring the alcohol down his throat, feeling the familiar burn as it made its way through his body and into his stomach.

Man that hit the spot. I deserve it. Being one helluva fucked up day. One drink never hurt anybody.

But if there was one thing for certain, Javier wasn't going to have just one drink. He never did anymore. It was always 'by the bottle' nowadays, and within the span of ten minutes, he had sucked down the entire bottle.

Can't believe I just did that, he though sadly, as he placed the tumbler back on the bar. Frustrated with himself for exhibiting such poor judgement on the job, he pushed it—a little too hard, and it slid across to the other side, landing on the floor with a thump.

The noise jarred the deputy, who looked around for the first time since he'd begun drinking.

The room seemed to sway and for a brief moment, went out of focus—appearing entirely differently. For a second, he could see a dusty bed and dresser. The floor was a dingy, green shag carpet and there were leaves piled up in various places around the room.

Shaking his head, Javier opened his eyes wider and tried to focus. Once again, the room appeared as it had initially—a saloon, with wooden paneled walls and fluorescent signs advertising different beer brands.

The old-school walkie-talkie phone on his hip suddenly crackled.

"Base to Cantra. Base to Cantra. Deputy Cantra, are you there?"

Javier pulled on the phone, and brought it up to his lips, "Cantra here. Can't find Rodriguez just yet. Checking on the inn. I think..."

As he spoke, the world shifted again and he suddenly found himself standing in a darkened, musty hotel room. The adjustment made him dizzy and he reached out to steady himself, accidentally dropping the phone.

"Deputy Cantra, are you there? I can't hear you."

Javier could hear the phone chirping at him, but he was feeling very dizzy.

And then, a light turned on in the bathroom.

What the fuck?

The door was nearly closed, with a small slit revealing the bright artificial white light inside. Javier squinted, trying to regain his bearings and felt icy pangs of fear when something black passed by the slit.

Holy shit. There's someone in there. Someone's been in this room the entire time I've been drinking. What if they tell someone? I could lose my badge.

With a shaking hand, he once again reached for the gun in his holster. Slowly removing it, Javier found his voice.

"I know you're in here. Come out slowly and there won't be any problems."

Meanwhile on the phone, Claire was getting increasingly concerned, "Deputy Cantra, do you need back-up?"

But Javier wasn't listening to her, because he was focused on the bathroom door and the light that was now shining brightly, hurting his eyes.

I drank too much. Shit. I should've left the bottle alone and done a careful sweep. I've been so stupid.

The light remained on in the bathroom, but the silence seemed unnatural. Javier turned around and to his horror, the bar was gone. It was replaced with an old-style television resting on a nightstand.

Creak

He swung back around and now the door to the bathroom was open. But the light was off.

The darkness looked like the mouth of a monster, ready to swallow him up.

"Hello?" his voice quivered.

No response.

Javier took a deep breath and walked slowly to the dark bathroom. It was impossible to see inside, so he reached around the doorframe and found the switch, flicking it on as quickly as he could while his gun was positioned straight ahead.

Terrified, he screamed, "Don't fuck with me! Come out or I'll have to shoot!"

He heard a slight rustling noise but to his surprise the bathroom appeared empty. From his vantage point he could see a basic sink with a mirror bolted to the wall. A customary tub with a shower curtain was at his left.

Javier reached out and pulled the curtain aside. The bathtub was empty.

The deputy was about to turn and leave when he felt the hairs on the back of his neck stand up. Out of his peripheral vision, he could see something black moving around on the ceiling. Slowly raising his gun, he turned to look up.

A hideous creature with the face of a hag, looked down and smiled at him. It was affixed to the ceiling with the legs of a spider and inverted feet. Black spindly fur covered its legs and to Javier's horror, it seemed like the individual strands were moving in synchronicity, swaying back and forth.

Javier's bladder suddenly emptied, and he urinated in his pants.

"What?" was all he could muster, before the creature leapt from the ceiling and landed on his head—crushing him as it tore his head apart.

10

Denise waited while Rod spoke to his communications officer. She looked across the street at the woods on the opposite side of the road and couldn't help but wonder if every minute they delayed was like a clock ticking down the seconds of her daughter's life.

A lump formed in her throat at the thought of Lilly. Her daughter had been missing for hours now, and she wondered if some perverted sicko had snatched her up and was now driving to Canada or to Mexico.

This isn't moving fast enough. We need to do something. Just standing here, dicking around isn't going to get us anywhere.

A feeling of panic swept over her, and Denise felt as if every nerve in her body was firing on all cylinders. She looked back and saw that Rod was pacing by the car, still deep in conversation on the phone.

Turning back to the street, Denise took a deep breath and began running toward the trees. She could hear Rod's confusion as he called out to her, but she didn't stop.

As she fled into the woods, Denise was immediately surrounded by tall trees and dense brush. She found herself pushing forward, convinced that Lilly was somewhere deep within the immense expanse of foliage. In the back of her mind, she knew that Rod was probably going to chase after her but she didn't care. She didn't care if he thought she was insane. Anything was better than remaining in one place and allowing her daughter to be pulled further and further away from her.

"Lilly! Lilly, are you out here?"

She could hear her voice literally dissipate in front of her face, carried away by the winds and rain that were sporadically assaulting her. The storm was beginning to blow through, rains attacking from the southeast as outer bands extended out, raking her face with wet tentacles.

The darkness was nearly absolute as Denise ran through the woods. She stumbled several times and nearly missed a branch hitting her squarely in the face. She knew that there was no clear compass to guide her through the unknown, yet she continued forward—calling for Lilly every time she paused.

I have to find her. Something's wrong. I can just feel it. Something's wrong.

Tears threatened to break through, and Denise tried to ignore the thought of something terrible happening to her daughter. She struggled to see into the darkness, when suddenly...

... she saw the embers of a dying fire in the distance.

What is that?

Denise struggled to maintain her composure, but the shroud of urgency draped over her shoulders, dragging her forward. She broke out into a sprint, racing toward the light—yelling as loud as she could, "Lilly! Lilly!"

A medium-sized boulder seemed to appear out of nowhere, and Denise tripped as her right foot struck it—sending her sprawling, face-forward into the dirt.

She put her hands out to cushion the blow and winced as the pain of various sticks and pebbles cut into her skin, leaving shallow lacerations.

Undeterred and ignoring the shooting pains erupting near and around her ankle, Denise pulled herself upright and continued forward, limping slightly as she moved toward the light.

Using nearby trees as support, she continued painstakingly forward, until she arrived at a clearing.

The fire had nearly died out within the rudimentary pit made of stone and sand. A series of logs surrounded the dying embers, and Denise could see that someone had left behind a small bowl that was now empty. A few stray ants chewed on the remainder of an almost finished meal.

But that was the only indication that anyone had been there. Lilly was nowhere to be found, and there were no clues as to which direction she'd gone. The darkness, wind and rain continued their assault, and Denise felt the strength in her aching legs disappear. She slowly sat down on one of the logs and began to cry.

Are you fucking kidding me?
Rod shook his head in disbelief.
She ran into the woods. Honestly. I know she's freaking out, but now I've got a serious situation on my hands. This is turning into a huge mess.
He considered reaching back out to Claire and then decided to deal with the situation first. There wasn't anything she could do anyway. And she was sending back-up, so he figured that at least someone could stay at the inn, in the event that the kid returned.

But Rod was starting to lose faith. Lilly had been gone for at least two hours, and he knew that without an Amber alert or any kind of watch notice, it would be difficult to find her.

But it's too soon to do anything just yet. I'd better go after Ms. Paskins. It's going to be rough in all this wind and rain.

Rod checked both ways, and then crossed the street. As he began to make his way into the woods, he saw a white figure cross the parking lot across the street and enter the inn.

That must be Javier. Glad he's here. He'll hold down the fort until I get back.

Rod was about to give Javier a call when he heard Denise call out for Lilly. Quickening his pace, he entered the darkness of the woods and turned on his flashlight for guidance through the maze of shrubbery, stones and stumps.

Unwilling to travel without one, Rod pulled a compass out of his pocket. Like most everyone on the squad, he also carried a smartphone (much to his wife's insistence), but years of cub scouts and camping had taught him that a compass was a wise tool to keep close. The woods he was entering went on for miles and miles—so getting lost wasn't just a possibility. It was highly likely. Particularly in the dark.

"Ms. Paskins?" he called out, well aware that she wasn't exactly wanting to be found as she continued in her manic, unrealistic search.

Rod was no psychologist, but he had some experience deal-ing with panicked parents. As the father of a five-year-old son, he could understand why a missing child created such severe and complex anxiety in an affected parent. He himself couldn't imagine how he would react if his own son was missing.

But Rod, despite understanding these reactions, also knew that this kind of anxiety could create roadblock and at times, even seriously hinder a search effort. On many occasions, affected parents were too panicked to calmly settle on a strategy that could lead to the most positive outcomes. They simply wanted to get back to their children as quickly as possible and therefore could have trouble with basic block and tackle techniques.

Denise running into the woods in search of her daughter didn't surprise him. Her actions had simply complicated matters because if her daughter was being held hostage by someone in the woods, this action may have now given the kidnapper ample notice that search and rescue was in full effect. In addition, he would now have to find mother and daughter, since they were both missing.

Or you could just turn around. The woman may be nuts and just trying to escape before you figure it out.

Rod shook his head and tried to ignore the small voice that questioned whether it was all worth it. He knew that the easy way out would be to just cancel the call, attributing the entire experience to an irrational, unstable woman.

After all, she took her supposed daughter to this inn and now this supposed daughter is missing. What if she doesn't exist and this woman is just off her rocker?

Rod stopped walking and stood still for a moment, trying to collect his thoughts.

It just doesn't make sense. If there is no daughter, why would this woman seem so panicked? No, she's legit. I've got to find her.

He started moving again and continued to search the area until he saw a light in the distance. It was dim, yellowish-orange and very hard to see. But there was no doubt in his mind that it was the result of a fire.

Moving more closely to the embers, he could hear the sounds of a woman sobbing.

Denise was sitting on a log. Her face was buried in her hands, and she cried softly. Her back heaved with each sob.

Rod felt his heart soften. It was never easy for him to see a woman cry. He didn't entirely know if she was telling the truth, but he felt his resolve begin to disappear. Regardless of what was going on, there was pain here. Lots of it.

He stepped forward carefully and knelt down beside her. Unsure of what to say, he remained in place, waiting for her to speak.

The sounds he made barely had an effect. Denise looked up slowly, and put her head back down. It was a relatively quick movement, but gave Rod enough time to see the rivers of tears that were flowing down her cheeks.

"I'm sorry," she whispered. "I didn't mean to run off like that. But I couldn't keep waiting. And I think she was here. Right in this spot. Someone has her. I just know it."

She's right. Why would there be a fire pit out here in the middle of nowhere? And those logs look like they've been pulled to this spot.

Instead of answering her, Rod surveyed the area—noticing the bowl lying by one of the logs. He walked around and pointed his flashlight on the ground, making a slow sweeping motion from left to right. It was difficult to see anything clearly because the rain was now misting down on them and the wind continued to carry items along the ground as it gusted loudly through the trees.

Suddenly, he saw it.

Footprints embedded in the muddy surface near the outskirts of the clearing. There were at least 3 different sizes heading in an easterly direction—back toward the inn.

To his disappointment, none of the prints were small enough to have come from a child, but that didn't mean that Lilly wasn't with them. He wondered if she was being carried.

Or dragged.

The thought gave him chills that he forced away.

The last thing I need right now is to frighten that poor woman. Something is definitely going on here. We can't keep going deeper into these woods. It looks like whoever was here is heading back in the direction that we came from. I wonder why we didn't see them?

A change in texture on one of the logs caught Rod's attention. He moved closer to it and saw that there was a powdery substance on the edge of the wood. Reaching down, he put his finger to it and took a closer look.

The powder was red and had a strange smell to it. It smelled like a mixture of burnt wood and something more … chemical.

He stood up slowly and felt more certain than ever that Denise was telling the truth.

Whoever was here had some kind of drug. And they may have used it on the child. Oh shit.

Denise was staring at him with wide, fearful eyes. "What is it? Did you find something?"

"Yes, I did. We need to retrace our steps back to the inn. And then, I need to call for more back-up."

11

As they entered the inn, the Elder wrinkled her forehead in disapproval. She could sense death nearby and knew that Sephira was to blame. There was such an anger in Sephira that didn't have an obvious origin and at times, the Elder wondered if she should have cast the woman out when the darkness first began to manifest.

It is too late now. She is a part of our coven. To release her from our circle would create far more problems than I am able to handle. My energy is so low lately. It is getting increasingly difficult to keep her under some form of control.

Despite her powers, Sephira was not much younger than the Elder. And she maintained a spell to keep up a youthful appearance around men. The Elder knew that in order to do this, Sephira would need to increasingly practice black magic because it would give her the strength to maintain the illusion. Regular magic was not powerful enough to support the constant source of energy needed to maintain the appearance of a raven-haired beauty.

"We must protect ourselves so that we are able to conduct our rituals in peace," the Elder said quietly. She rarely spoke aloud, but her coven sisters were always quick to respond. This time, Sephira—who had been waiting for them at the inn and now came forward—was the one to respond.

She tossed her black hair and spoke brazenly, "I'll do it. This is a perfect opportunity for me to practice a series of spells that I've been working on. Allow me the responsibility, dear Elder."

"Are you capable of maintaining the area? So much of your strengths have gone into ... other things."

Sephira's eyes narrowed. She didn't like to be questioned and knew that the Elder was very wise. But she felt confident in her abilities.

"Yes," she said bluntly. "This is no problem. I'll make things very difficult for anyone who stands in our way."

The Elder watched as Sephira moved quickly past them and

ascended the stairs. *She is full of anger and blackness. The energy around us doesn't feel entirely right. But there is no choice. We must press on. This is the evening of the change and the child must be fully indoctrinated.*

Nyssa was carrying Lilly now, and the Elder was pleased to see that the child was resting peacefully. The spells and invisible powders used to sedate the girl were harmless enough and would be absorbed by the body in due time.

One of the downstairs windows rattled suddenly, as a gust of rain-filled wind thrashed the building—a reminder that the outskirts of the storm were impacting the town.

The Elder could sense that the time was drawing near. "Ok, let's get the child upstairs. Sephira will protect us."

And I feel sorry for anyone who gets in her way.

12

Nyssa ascended the stairs as carefully as she could. The child, despite not being very large was still relatively heavy and felt heavier with each step.

She was surprised at how much the Countryside Inn had deteriorated over the years. Its walls were cracked and worn, layers of dust resting on the surfaces. Sephira had been casting a strong spell over the building to make it appear new and had even fabricated an innkeeper to maintain the illusion. Nyssa knew that wasn't an easy task to pull off and was impressed that Sephira had been so successful. Otherwise, securing the child would have been difficult.

Secretly, Nyssa wondered if Sephira had become too brazen. She was around the same age as her fellow witches, and yet, Nyssa had watched her change ... evolving into a creature of very few boundaries. Sephira was using dark magic regularly and at times, it had become a problem. Especially when she chose to practice on the local townsfolk.

Throughout the years, the coven had worked tirelessly to remain anonymous. With the advent of witch-fandom coupled with the years-old discrimination of anything witch-like, all it would take were a couple of small mistakes for their identities to be revealed. The coven had remained hidden for hundreds of years, with witches teaching their sisters the secrets and the ways of magic. There was a lot at stake. And Nyssa felt that Sephira was putting them all at risk.

The Elder had been keeping a watchful eye on the group, especially since they were now all at an advanced age and new life was needed to keep the group viable. Within about five years, there would be a need for additional recruits. Efforts were underway to search for the next of kin, similarly to the way they had found Lilly. Manipulating her mother's computer had been easy. She'd been in panic mode, trying to find a safe place to stay and had fallen squarely into their trap.

Lilly was very important to them.

Even now, Nyssa could feel the strength from the child permeating her skin. She knew that true witches weren't touched by genetics or hereditary factors. Instead, they had been chosen through a series of divine intervention stretching centuries back. There were age-old books written that contained the secrets of the children who would be touched by the spirit.

While Lilly's parents were not chosen ones, the time of their daughter's conception, coupled with their location, the numbers dictating the date and time of birth, and the mapped coordinates of the location where Lilly was born were the key indicators that led them to the proper target.

It was not a perfect science however, and there had been mistakes with children they'd chosen in the past. But now … now they were certain that they'd found their next sister and within a short period of time their ritual would finalize this new adoption.

Dark shadows lurked in the corners and Nyssa could see oddities in her peripheral vision. Despite knowing that Sephira was behind the darkness that was surrounding them now, it was still frightening. Nyssa wasn't comfortable with the depths of the darkness that surrounded her sisters and felt a chill as dark and strange shapes began growing on the walls.

Sephira glided effortlessly around the inn, feeling a charge every time she concocted a new dark spell. It was thrilling to see the horrific creatures emerge from the dark, their mad eyes wet with anger, their bodies slick with vile phlegm.

They are my powerful babies, doing my bidding.

She laughed as her body moved through the air, only pausing when she came to a mirror.

Frowning, she noticed that new wrinkles had appeared around her eyes and mouth. And there were now silver strands, standing out starkly against the blackness of her hair. Sephira could feel the beginnings of fatigue start to work their way into her core.

Better be careful. Don't want to use up all of my energy. But can't look like shit in the process either.

Squeezing her hands into fists, Sephira bore down and

focused on the spell that would keep her youthful. As she repeated the spell in her mind, there was a flash and she though that her creatures had disappeared momentarily. But when he opened her eyes, they were all around her—awaiting further instruction.

She laughed loudly, and chastised herself for worrying. The woman now staring back at her in the mirror was one of beauty and youth.

Sephira snorted and floated out of the room, heading back to rejoin the others. She felt confident about the world she'd created inside the inn.

Lilly felt weightless as if floating through air. She could feel her body move through space and time, but there was no effort in the movement. Her mind was hazy and calm.

Where am I? It smells weird—kinda like burning wood.

The child lifted her head and looked around. She was moving through the air and all around her, fog and fires stretched for as far as her eyes could see. Lilly squinted and tried to focus. Her movement had stopped but now there was something floating in the air in front of her.

It was a pair of eyes. But these eyes were larger than any eyes she'd ever seen. And they were purple, blinking slowly and as regularly.

"What are you?" Lilly could feel herself asking without moving her mouth.

"My name is everything," a bodiless voice responded. It was a female voice, and it sounded like a teenager. This immediately put Lilly at ease. She tried to focus on the voice and knew that somehow, this conversation was very important.

"Where are you taking me?" she asked.

Instead of responding, the eyes softened and blinked. "Are you afraid?"

"No, I'm not scared. But I want to know what's going on. Are you going to take me somewhere bad?"

"We are part of you. You are a part of us. This is part of your destiny. It will make sense very soon. You are not in danger."

The voice sounded reassuring, and Lilly lowered her head.

She could still see the fog and the fires burning in the distance. But she was no longer afraid and embraced the darkness that once again took over her mind.

As Nyssa neared the ritual room, she could feel Lilly begin to shift in her arms. She wasn't surprised. The Mother spoke to all new sisters prior to the ritual. It was part of becoming melded with the coven. And it was a test that had no right or wrong answer. The Mother would know if the child was a true witch or an imposter.

13

Claire was nervous. It wasn't like Javier to not respond to her texts, calls or two-way radio attempts. She'd been trying to reach him for nearly a half hour, unsuccessfully. To top it off, she hadn't been able to reach Rod either. The last time she's connected with him, it had been more than an hour before—and he'd indicated that he was going to search the woods for a missing child.

A gust of wind rattled the window next to her desk.

Damn. This storm is settling in. We may not be getting the full blast but we're still getting some of it. Hope the power doesn't go off.

Claire decided to try and reach Rod again, with a less formal and more urgent communication. She decided to text:

Rod, where are you? I can't reach Javier at all. Starting to get worried. There's no one near you guys who I can send out. Need confirmation that things are ok. Please respond within the next five minutes. — Claire.

Unable to sit still, Claire stretched and walked over to the coffee pot. She'd been drinking the wet tar all night, and was still exhausted.

She'd begun pouring more coffee into her cup when the phone on her desk rang, causing her to spill some of the hot liquid on to the table.

"Shit!" She quickly put the cup on the counter and ran to the phone.

"Hello?" she answered quickly, and without her customary and mandated greeting.

The line was full of static. Claire could hear someone on the line and strained her ears, trying to make out what was being said.

"I'm sorry, I can't hear you. Rod is that you? Javier? Who is it?"

"Claire … street … inn … send … out."

It was impossible for her to make out any additional words, but the voice was definitely Rod's.

"Hello? Hello? Rod? Are you still there?"

The static suddenly stopped and then … a loud scream pierced her ears with a shrill intensity.

Claire dropped the phone on the table, her hands shaking from surprise.

Pull it together. Pick up the phone. Someone's in trouble.

With a trembling hand, Claire slowly picked up the receiver. But now, the line was dead.

Thoughts raced through her mind. She'd never been in a situation before where there was no backup, no one to call, no clear way to handle the respective situation laid out before her.

Something's happening out there. Can't reach anyone, can't get anyone to call me back. And this weather's really bad too.

She looked out the window and stared at the trees swaying to and fro and the gusts of rain blowing through intermittently—typical of outlying tropical storm rain bands.

There's something about that inn. That place should've been torn down a while ago. It never made any real money, and now it just sits out there. Rotting.

The inn had been a part of the town for as long as Claire could remember. When she was a child, her aunt had stayed there over a weekend, while attending a cousin's wedding. Claire remembered her mother pulling up the gravel driveway and parking the car, dust kicking up around them.

Inside, the Countryside Inn didn't look all that fancy, and instead—the sparse furniture appeared worn and dated. The most interesting item in the room was a painting on the wall of a location deep within the woods, with a spot of red-orange flames in the distance, and a dark shadow looming above the trees.

The painting was strange and unsettling. Claire recalled how she couldn't help but stare at it, even with the way it made her feel. It was like she was hypnotized as the trees pulled her in tighter and tighter…

Eventually, her aunt had come downstairs and they'd left. But Claire could still remember how empty the inn had seemed to her and how strange she'd felt inside the old place.

Then, there were the rumors around town that once the

inn had closed down due to financial troubles, it had become a haven for drunk teenagers and Satan worshippers. Claire wasn't sure she believed all of that but some people claimed that lights went on in the building at odd hours of the night. She'd even called out for a deputy to check it out after someone had called saying that a woman was sitting in one of the windows, staring out at the street.

Of course, the patrolman at the time hadn't found anything when he'd gone out. Though he did seem a bit nervous over the radio and didn't care to talk about it later on.

When Claire had asked him about the inn, he'd simply answered, "There wasn't anything there. And it's a good thing they shut that place down. It's not a nice place. Old, dusty and not really somewhere I'd want to pay to be."

It was a weird answer to a very simple question. But Claire had chosen not to probe. After all, he'd checked it out and hadn't found anything, so it was time to move on and worry about the next issue.

Now, however, she wondered if there was something more going on.

I can't just sit here. What if Rod and Javier are in trouble?

Decision made, Claire grabbed her keys off the counter, snatched a rain slicker off a nearby coat hanger and headed out the door.

14

The wind and rain had started picking up, but Denise barely noticed. She couldn't forget the look on the deputy's face when he'd noticed a powdery substance near the dying fire.

He'd looked frightened.

Since then, he hadn't spoken—not even a word. Instead, he'd walked ahead of her and was moving very quickly ... almost too fast for her to keep up.

And it was slow going. The grass and stones on the ground were wet, and it was difficult to maintain balance. A few times, Denise had slipped and saved herself from falling by using nearby branches or limbs for support. Her ankle still ached from her earlier stumble, but it wasn't too bad.

The wind had the trees in a constant dance, and Denise had to duck a few times to avoid getting scratched by prickly branches.

"Hey, can you slow down?" she gasped.

Rod didn't respond and continued to push forward. His boots easily navigated the wet terrain, giving him a strong stride.

When they finally made it to the outskirts of the woods, Denise felt a surge of relief. Even with the howling winds around them, being within the dense foliage was stifling, and she was glad to be on the other side.

Rod finally turned and looked back at her. "You ok?"

Denise tried to smile and pushed wet strands of hair off her face. "Yeah, I'm ok. Look!"

Even from the other side of the road, it was easy to see that light was shining from inside the inn. In fact, all the windows were lit from the inside.

"Let's go!" Denise shouted, and pushed past Rod toward the street. But as soon as she tried to cross the road, she felt a shock. Her body flew backward as if pushed by an invisible assailant.

Rod rushed over to her. "Are you ok?"

Aside from some scratches on her elbows, and a bruised

rear-end, Denise felt ok. "Yeah, I'm ok. But what the hell was that?"

Rod looked back toward the road. "I'm not sure. One minute you were rushing ahead and the next minute, you were falling backwards. Did you trip over something? What happened?"

Denise shook her head. "I'm not sure. But be careful. Something didn't let me get on the road."

Rod wiped his eyes, which were stinging from the sweat and rain. Nothing was making sense.

"Ok, let me try." He walked to the edge of the grass and slowly put out his foot. As he began to lower it, a tingling sensation began and then started to get worse and worse until he could no longer stand it. He then moved a bit farther north and then a bit farther south. But no matter what he tried, he could not put his foot on the ground without getting a shock.

"This makes no sense. How can I not cross the street?"

Denise, who was now sitting on the grass—not caring that her pants were getting wet or dirty—shook her head again.

"Something doesn't want us to get to the other side."

Rod wondered if he was going crazy, because things were just getting worse and worse—without any clear explanation.

No matter how hard he tried, he couldn't stop his foot from getting shocked when he brought it close to the road.

This is ridiculous. Maybe if we walk a mile or so in either direction we can get across. Not sure if that is going to help though. We've got to get across more quickly than that.

Just then, a rock whizzed past his face and into the road. It bounced a few times on the street in front of them and stopped.

"See? Other things can get across! It's just us!" Denise was beginning to get panicked.

"Alright, let's think this through. Let me give Claire a call at headquarters to see if she can help us. And please, no more rocks."

Reaching for his phone, Rod wondered if maybe a powerline was down nearby and was causing static electricity so strong that it had created a force field of some kind. That was the only explanation he could come up with that made any sense at all.

He was irritated (but not entirely surprised) to see that he had only one bar of reception on his phone. Shaking his head, he quickly dialed the station.

To his disappointment, it rang a handful of times and then a rarely-used voice message responded back—meaning that no one was able to answer the phone at the station.

"Claire, it's Rod. We're stuck on the side of the street. We can't get to the other side. It's really bizarre. We're not sure what to do. We need you to send some back-up to help us get out. We're still trying to find Ms. Paskin's daughter. Call me…"

The phone in his hand suddenly went dead. The battery, which had seemed fine moments ago was now entirely drained. The rain had stopped momentarily, but the winds battered his face from both sides.

This damned electrical barrier. I'll bet it drained my entire battery. Shit. There wasn't enough rain to do anything like this to my phone. This is insane!

Denise was looking up at him expectantly. "So, is help coming?"

Rod didn't answer and turned to face the inn. He could see movement in one of the windows and felt a bad sensation in his gut that time was running out.

The rain was intermittent but the wind was constant. Claire could feel her car involuntarily moving into the wrong lane and fought to keep control of the steering wheel.

Thankfully most people were off the road, giving her room to course correct every time she felt a gust of air push on her vehicle. Street and business lights flickered periodically—the town's electrical grid taking a beating.

And we're not even getting the hurricane. It's really battering Florida. That woman must have barely reached Georgia before this other storm hit us. They say that both of these storms are moving really fast.

Claire wasn't sure why their town was getting such massive amounts of wind and rain so quickly, but without time to watch the local news or scroll through her phone, she simply accepted that it was either a system connected to the hurricane or another one that was impacting their part of the country.

She maneuvered her car as carefully as possible to handle the winding roads. Heavily wooded areas flanked the sides of the street as the landscape became less populated and wilder.

Finally, she saw the Countryside Inn up ahead. Strangely, there were lights on inside the building. A lump formed in her throat.

What the hell is going on? Did they suddenly get electricity? That makes no sense.

Doing her best to maintain control of the car, Claire slowed down considerably and parked her vehicle behind Rod's cruiser. She sat behind the wheel for a few moments and looked around—feeling safer in the locked car.

Rain continued to fall and every so often a gust of wind would shake the car slightly. But other than the natural disturbances caused by the storm, there didn't seem to be anyone else around. This seemed odd, because Claire felt as if there were people watching her.

Shaking off the strange sensations, she got out of the car and opened up an umbrella, taking in the surrounding area.

The darkness made it difficult to see anything, and other than the blazing lights emanating from the inn's windows, there wasn't much else to focus on.

I could go searching into the woods, but I would probably get lost. There's lights on inside the inn. My chances of finding people there are much better.

As Claire ascended the steps toward the front door of the building, she could hear music and voices on the other side of the wall.

What in the hell is going on? There's no way they opened up this old place for a hurricane party! Those people have to be trespassing. Maybe it's a bunch of drunken teenagers and Rod's in there dealing with them. Oh, they better watch out. I'm in a shitty mood and this weather ain't helping.

Feeling a surge of irritation push through her, Claire threw the door open and prepared to help handle some unruly people.

But when the door swung ajar, she couldn't believe what she was seeing.

The Countryside Inn was full of people.

Men and women, wearing attire that was fashionable in the 1970s occupied the 1st floor of the building. A waiter walked around, offering up bottles of beer and flutes filled with a bubbly liquid. Groups of people stood together laughing and talking loudly. A short line of people stood by the reception area, some of them with suitcases resting on the ground as they chatted with a young woman who stood behind the counter.

The furniture and accompanying paintings were earth-toned, with paintings of the forest lining the walls. In one of the paintings, Claire could see a group of elderly women sitting around a bonfire. They were all hunched over and the woods behind them were depicted in a dark, threatening black.

Despite throwing the door open, none of the people inside the inn seemed to take much notice of her, leaving Claire momentarily feeling lightheaded and confused. She looked wildly around the room, searching for anything remotely familiar, but the jubilant party continued around her as if she didn't exist.

Fuck this. I need answers.

"Deputy Rodriguez! Rod! Are you in here?" Claire shouted at the top of her lungs.

The music and all the sounds in the room stopped suddenly. Each person turned to look at her in unison.

"We're all here. Everything's ok. We're all here."

Their voices sounded like a recording—distant and monotone.

Dead.

Rod felt a surge of relief when lights from an oncoming car came into view. It was difficult at first to identify who was behind the wheel, but as the car came closer, he recognized the vehicle as Claire's car and could see her determined face as she slowly turned and parked behind his cruiser.

Rod liked Claire. A lot. While he'd been nursing his recent divorce, Claire had been a helpful friend, listening to him talk about what had gone wrong and what he was hoping for in a relationship. Through their talks and friendly lunches, he'd found that she possessed a warm, natural type of beauty that really grew on a person. In truth, he'd been hoping to ask her out on a date, but the right time hadn't presented itself.

If we get through this, I will definitely ask her out. I've wasted enough time.

Behind him, Denise slowly rose to her feet. "Oh thank goodness. Let's call out to her, and see if that woman can help us get across the street."

Rod could see Claire get out of the car and then hesitate, as if she was aware of their presence.

"Claire! Claire! We're over here."

She looked around and even stared straight at him, before turning back around.

"Why isn't she saying anything to us?" Denise asked, her voice quivering as if she already knew the answer.

Rod shook his head. "I don't know. It's all very strange. I mean, I just called out to her and she looked right at me. But it was like she couldn't see me at all."

Denise didn't answer, and instead—dropped her head into her hands and started crying softly.

This is a nightmare, Rod thought to himself. *There's got to be a way out of this mess.*

Claire stood still for a moment, not able to fully accept what was happening.

After the odd proclamation from the partygoers, they stared at her for a moment and then resumed their discussions. The music began to play and ambient party sounds of glasses clinking and people chatting filled the air once more.

This must be some sort of hallucination. There's no way this is happening. This place has been closed for years. And these people look like they're either having a costume party or they've just stepped out of the 1970s. Either way, I've got to figure out where my deputies are. They've both been missing for at least an hour now. Something's going on.

Trying to move as inconspicuously as possible, Claire slowly wove her way around the strange people until she was able to make it out of the room and found herself in the foyer that led to the stairwell. She put her hand on the banister when suddenly the ground shifted underneath her and everything went dark.

"Hello?" she called out, now terrified.

Silence answered and in the distance, rain flew against the windows, making a rat-tat-tat sound.

Unable to see behind her and unsure of what might be following, Claire decided to continue forward and stepped into the stairwell. Once she was closer to the stairs she could see lights flickering ahead.

A series of candles were set up individually in sconces that lined the wall. The air was musty and warm, and Claire could occasionally hear the wind howling outside and wrapping its wet tentacles around the building.

She stared down at her cell phone, and punched in the number to the state trooper's station.

All I need to do is hit SEND. It's not a great back-up plan, but it's something.

Feeling weakness in her legs, Claire slowly ascended the stairs, noticing that everything around her had become dusty and worn out. It seemed now more like what she remembered.

A deserted, dusty abandoned building.

Not wanting to take any chances, she moved more quickly and finally reached the second floor.

Lilly felt calm. She knew that the woman who carried her was a stranger, and that the women who surrounded her had odd names and old faces. They didn't speak to her and instead, walked side-by-side and chanted a song in low voices.

The night is upon us,
This time of choosing dear Mother,
We are eternally grateful for your love and guidance,
As you send a flame and embrace the other.

We sing to you in passion and trust,
You have the key to what will be,
Time is drawing near and close,
To decide on the fate of the chosen key.

It was a soulful melody that Lilly found soothing and strangely familiar. She started closing her eyes, when she felt Nyssa shift.

"It's time. I'm going to put you on the bed now. Don't worry. You're safe with us."

Lilly felt her body being lowered on to a mattress. It was soft and everything around her smelled like the incense her mother sometimes burned during lazy evenings at home.

At the thought of her mother, Lilly felt a pang of sorrow. She knew that by now, her disappearance had to have everyone panicked – her mother most of all.

I really should try to get away. That would be the thing Mom would expect me to do. She always wants me to be responsible. So why am I not doing what she would want? Why are my legs so tired? Why do I feel so sleepy? And these people—they feel safe to me. They don't feel like strangers.

Lilly tried to open her eyes wider, but each eyelid felt heavy.

"Where is Mom?" she whispered.

The same gentle voice responded, "Your mother is fine, Lilly. You mustn't worry. Right now, just rest. Soon, you will be a part of something very special. This is something you were meant to be a part of for a very long time. You are unique. In time, you will be one of us. The hour is drawing near. You are safe, and we will protect you."

Lilly didn't understand what she was being told but she also didn't have any energy to argue or to pose any questions. Instead, she closed her eyes and allowed sleep to take over once more.

15

Denise felt as if her entire world was crumbling around her. She felt her tears fall and wet the palms that cradled the immense weight of her head.

How can this be happening? My daughter is missing, we're stuck on one side of the road… It's like we're invisible. But I'm not invisible. I'm right here! This isn't a dream. There has to be a way out of this. What if someone has my child and is harming her? How can I do anything when I'm frozen in place? This can't be the end of everything. I can't just sit here and let this happen. I've got to do something.

A surge of determination filling her veins, Denise stood up. Brushing the tears from her face, she stared straight ahead into the road and before she could even fully comprehend what she was doing, she raced forward into the street.

Her body propelled itself ahead and in the distance, she could hear Rod shout.

"Denise, stop!"

But she didn't stop. Instead, Denise ran forward with all of her might and closed her eyes, bracing herself for the invisible wall that would prevent her from reaching the other side.

But it never came.

Instead, she felt the gravel and the bituminous surface of the road against her shoes as she ran to the other side of the street. She stopped short of Rod's car, heaving and out of breath.

Looking across the street, Denise could see the deputy staring at her, a confused look on his face.

"Come on," she shouted. "You can do it! I think whatever was blocking us has disappeared!"

Rod hesitated and then ran across the street with a determined look on his face. He too was able to freely cross the road and made his way over to where Denise was standing.

"What the hell?" he asked, his resolve clearly shaken.

"It doesn't matter anymore," Denise answered. "We've got to go in there and save Lilly. I know she's somewhere in there. I can just feel it."

Rod nodded. "Me too. But we've got to be careful. We can't just go bursting in. You know things haven't exactly been normal tonight, agreed?"

"I know what you mean. But we've got to do something quickly. What's your plan?"

The deputy hesitated for a moment and then looked up at the building. The windows were dark with the exception of rain drops that reflected the moonlight up ahead.

"We go in carefully. And we stick together. No matter what."

Denise nodded.

The two slowly walked up the steps toward the front door. Neither commented on the additional car in the driveway. The car was off, and Rod figured that Claire was still inside. But the lights in the building were off, which didn't exactly provide heaps of confidence that she was ok.

Either way, they weren't stopping.

Rod reached out and slowly turned the knob at the front door. It moved easily in his hands, and rotated—revealing darkness inside and a wall.

"What the hell?" Rod muttered under his breath.

The entire first floor was blocked by a short hallway that turned to the right.

It was a maze.

"You've gotta be kidding me," Denise whispered. "What the hell is going on here? How did someone put this thing in the middle of the hotel? This doesn't make any sense."

Rod wondered if the problem they'd experienced in crossing the street had somehow extended to the Countryside Inn. It was a crazy thought, but he had no other explanation for the walls that now blocked their immediate search for Lilly.

"We don't have much choice. We've just got to follow the path until we can find the stairs. I don't think there's anything or anyone down here."

Denise shut the door.

"Ok, let's go."

Sephira was beginning to feel signs of fatigue. Despite the importance of the moment, and Lilly's utter compliance to the ritual being performed—she could feel that her magic was being tested.

She'd set several spells in motion to delay any intrusion or interruption. But there were now several life forces pulling on the energy of her magic, and she feared that this new development had weakened the spells, making some of them ineffective.

In addition, the drain on her powers was causing her appearance to begin to fade into its reality. Liver spots were appearing along her arms, and Sephira was afraid that her face was beginning to lose it luster.

Some of the other women had been shooting glances her way, and it gave Sephira an inkling as to what was going on.

"We're running out of time," she hissed to the Elder. "My magic is powerful, but I'm only one soul. Can some of the other sisters help me out here?"

The Elder, who was reciting the prayers of the moon change, looked at her for a moment and shook her head.

Sephira wasn't surprised. It would take the strength of all in the coven to ensure that the transition was successful. The Elder couldn't take the chance of losing any momentum.

And the other witches simply weren't as strong.

Sephira sighed loudly. She knew that her magic wouldn't last forever.

I should just kill that stupid child. Why do we need another member of the coven right now? She'll just grow older, stronger and more powerful than I'll ever be. And we're taking all of this risk. Doing a conversion ceremony in the middle of a storm when all of these damned people are around. We should have taken her deep into the woods somewhere. That would've been the smart thing to do. Instead, we're stuck in this cramped room, where we're all trapped if someone comes in and starts to shoot at us. And if we don't complete the ceremony soon—I'll be too weak and powerless to fight back.

She glared at Lilly who now lay completely still on the bed. Anger—hot and permeating—flooded Sephira's mind. Snarling, she felt the need to pounce and pull the child's throat out.

Suddenly, a hand rested on her arm … and then a second one … and a third one…

The sisters were connected by more than just the coven. They could sense each other, feel when the energy had taken a different turn. And Sephira's anger was palpable, causing the others to move in and ensure that nothing was done to interrupt the ceremony.

Sephira took a deep breath and tried to calm the anger inside of her. The realization that her sisters would never allow anything to happen to the child was clear now. She would have to be as strong as possible, while keeping her magic alive to protect them.

And when this is all over, I may choose to kill that creature anyway. On my own time, she thought. The mere idea caused her to snicker evilly.

16

Claire stood at the 2nd floor entrance in disbelief.

Instead of a normal hallway with a beginning and an end, the hallway before her seemed infinite. It continued on and on … only darkness in the distance.

And every door looked exactly the same.

Old, dusty and foreboding.

Shit. What do I do now? There are people up here—I just know it. Maybe they're hiding.

In her head, Claire could hear the voice of her mother, warning her that exploring a dark hallway in the middle of the night, in the middle of nowhere—was definitely not a good idea.

"You really want to do this? Claire, honey, this is a big mistake. You should just go downstairs, get away from all of this nonsense, get back in your car, and go back to work. It isn't your job to go patrolling around danger. We didn't bring you up to make such bad decisions. You're smarter than this. Time to let the professionals do their job."

Despite everything, Claire smiled.

Yes. My mother would definitely not approve of this. I can't believe I'm taking such a risk. But these deputies are my friends. I can't just leave them here to deal with this. Time to put on my big-girl panties and figure this shit out.

Claire pointed her flashlight straight ahead and to her dismay, the light extended out a bit and then was swallowed up by the thick darkness ahead. Taking a deep breath, she pursed her lips and took a few steps forward.

The howling wind roared in the distance, and Claire could hear the inn creak and rattle in displeasure.

Turning to her right, she decided to try one of the doors. Reaching out, Claire grasped a cold metal knob and found that it wouldn't turn.

"Locked. Damn," she whispered aloud.

Something or someone giggled behind her.

Claire swung the flashlight around and to her horror, the

stairwell had disappeared and a long dark hallway was in its place.

"Hello? Is anyone there?"

Another soft giggle and then...

Claire was able to make out a small figure in the distance. It looked like a child, but she couldn't be absolutely certain.

Squinting, she took a few steps forward. "Are you ok? I'm looking for a policeman."

The figure didn't reply and remained in place.

Icy fingers of fear began to wrap themselves around Claire's heart, and she began to think about running.

Then, the lights flew on and Claire found that the image had disappeared and she was standing in a lit hallway that still seemed infinite on both sides. Now, however, people walked in and out of bedrooms talking to one another.

The same type of people she had seen downstairs—people who looked as if they'd stepped out of the 1970s.

Claire thought about trying to stop one of them, asking for help but decided against it. Instead, she stood and watched until she saw a woman enter one of the bedrooms and quickly followed her before the door shut.

The woman breezed into a room where a man waited on the bed for her. He was dressed in a brown suit but had begun removing his tie and jacket.

Neither the man nor woman seemed to notice Claire, so she didn't feel it was necessary to hide and sat on a chair—watching the scene in front of her unfold as if it was a movie.

The woman seemed tired and, sitting on the edge of the bed, took off her heels and began rubbing her feet.

"Walter, what a great time. It was so groovy to see everyone. Did you enjoy yourself?"

Walter had now taken off his jacket and undershirt. His chest was hairy and built.

Claire thought he was kind of attractive, in an old-school kind of way.

"It was alright," he answered in a Southern drawl. "Would've preferred to watch football. These things are kinda silly. Everyone tryin' to outdo each other."

The woman started at him with a blank look on her face, and then resumed rubbing her feet.

Walter on the other hand, had now removed his pants and was now only wearing his underwear. He scratched at his crotch absentmindedly and started at the woman.

It was pretty obvious to Claire that Walter was started to get interested in more than just bland conversation.

"Why don'tcha come over here and we'll have our own little party?" he asked, while tugging on his growing bulge.

The woman smiled—though Claire thought she looked a bit odd—almost as if the smile was covering up something else.

Instead of responding, the woman stretched out on the bed and began kissing Walter. They began to squirm against each other until the woman was straddling Walter. She was still wearing her clothes, and looked as if she was going to start taking off her top when she reached across the nightstand and grasped something that Claire couldn't quite identify … and then she drove it down into Walter's throat.

It was a knife.

Claire shrieked and jumped out of her chair, backing up—the strange reverie she'd been pulled into—now broken.

Blood spurted out of the wound in Walter's neck and sprayed all over the woman's face. She turned to face Claire.

"Isn't it just groovy?" she asked, blood dripping down her pale face.

Her mouth stretched down, revealing jagged, uneven teeth.

Claire screamed and raced of out of the room, pulling the door shut behind her.

Rod was exhausted and extremely frustrated. They'd been following the maze and seemed to be going in circles. And on top of everything else, he had to take a piss. He'd been trying to ignore the nagging sensation in his bladder for a bit, but it was just getting impossible and it needed immediate attention.

Denise looked tired too. He figured that maybe it was a good time to take a quick bio-break.

Stopping, he put his hands on his hips and leaned up against a wall.

"Hey, do you mind if I step around the corner and take a quick break? I've got to relieve myself, and I'd prefer not to do it in front of you."

Denise nodded. "Just do it in a spot behind where we are, so we don't have to step over it as we go."

"Sure, no problem. Just wait here, and I'll be right back."

He walked a bit, and turned down a hallway that they'd already visited. Turning around to be sure Denise was not within eyeshot, he paused and then quickly removed his holster.

After a bit of maneuvering, Rod was able to position himself away from view and urinated fast and hard, watching the stream hit the ground in the darkness.

In the midst of relieving himself, Rod became aware of a sizzling sound. It sounded at first like eggs cooking on a skillet, but matched the intensity and speed of his urine stream.

He quickly finished up and the grabbed his flashlight that was lying on the ground, pointing it at the direction of the sound.

To his surprise, Rod could now see a hole in the wall ... it wasn't far from the puddle he'd made and looked large enough for a person to easily pass through.

"Denise," he called out. "Come here, quick!"

He waited until she appeared around the corner and pointed his flashlight at the hole.

"I think we should go through there."

Denise stared at the hole, her eyes wide with disbelief. "How the hell did that appear there? Did you pee acid or something?"

The question was ridiculous, and both of them chuckled.

"No, not quite," Rod said, becoming serious once more. "I don't know how it got there, but I think it's worth trying. We've been walking through this maze, and it doesn't seem to be getting us anywhere."

Denise was hesitant. She stepped closer to the hole and tried to shine her flashlight inside. But it was impossible to see what was on the other side. It was too dark and all she could see was the ground and a large space on the other side.

"I'm scared," she admitted. "We need to find my daughter, it's just that this whole situation is so fucked up. Don't know what to do."

Rod reached out and gently touched her shoulder.

"I understand how you're feeling. This is beyond anything I've ever dealt with as well. But we can't keep walking through a maze. I'm not sure where this hole will lead us. Shit, we've got to take a chance. Nothing is normal here."

Denise turned away, tears now running down her cheeks.

Rod could tell that she was terrified and couldn't blame her. He was very uneasy as well and wondered what lay on the other side of the mysterious hole.

"Ok, let's do it."

Sephira felt a sharp pain in her side as one of her spells weakened suddenly, causing her to focus suddenly on the magic that was beginning to fade.

It was her infinite maze that had suffered a setback and she feared that there were people testing the boundaries of the trap she'd set for them.

"Are you ok?" Nyssa whispered.

"I'm fine," Sephira hissed, "just feeling a little tired. If one of you could help me keep these spells in place, I would be in a much better place. Instead, you're more focused on this stupid child. She won't be able to help us if a bunch of people show up and attack us."

The Elder shot Sephira a warning look, and Nyssa stepped back as if physically attacked.

"How can you say such an awful thing? We are in the process of inducting this child into our sisterhood. Shortly, she will become one of us. One of our own. She has been chosen. How can you have such spitefulness toward a part of your coven?"

The irritated witch threw her head back, and laughed. She was aging quickly now and white streaks lined her hair. Her voice was changing as well, and becoming increasingly scratchy—the seductive tone disappearing with the power of her magic.

"I don't need anyone to feel sisterhood. You are all a part of me and that's why I remain here tonight, conducting this ritual to add to our numbers. My magic is keeping us safe, and that brings me pleasure. But don't for a minute think that I care about this child. She is not at the same level as us. Continue your praying and singing. I'll focus on the magic that protects our circle. And please, keep your patronizing bullshit to yourself."

Sephira leaned over and ran a finger over Lilly's cheek. She knew that her actions were angering the Elder and was finding it refreshing that she didn't give a rat's ass one way or the other.

17

Claire continued running until her legs ached and the air burned in her lungs. The hallway just seemed to go on and on and no matter how long she ran, she couldn't reach the end of it.

She stopped and gasped for air as sweat dripped down her face.

Holy shit. What am I going to do? There doesn't seem to be anyone chasing me but I've been running and running and this hallway never seems to end. Am I going to be stuck in here forever, trying to open doors that won't open?

Reaching in her pocket, Claire pulled out her phone. As she expected, there was no signal. She tried to send a text to her mother, but the message didn't deliver.

Ok, this isn't good. Think, Claire, think!

She looked around. The hallway was long, with doors flanking each side. Each door looked exactly the same, only now there weren't any people walking around.

Well, one of these doors opened before, so maybe I just need to try again.

Walking over to the closest door, Claire reached out with trembling fingers and grasped the knob. It remained firmly in place and didn't turn at all.

Sighing, frustration mounting, Claire walked over to the next door. She reached out again, when she suddenly felt lightheaded and everything around her ... flickered. And for a brief moment she was standing in the center of a dark, dusty hallway that ended after a series of rooms.

"What the hell?" She couldn't believe her eyes.

The hallway was once again infinite and dimly lit. Claire tried rubbing her eyes and pinching herself, wondering if everything that was happening around her was simply a bad dream.

When everything remained the same and Claire felt more confident to proceed, she decided to reach for the nearest door again. As her hand connected with the knob, she was surprised when the metal fixture slowly turned and there was a click as the door opened.

Uncertain as to what she would find this time, Claire gently opened the door and slowly stepped inside.

This room was dark, with the exception of a lit lamp next to the bed. There was a strange glow coming from the window that flickered in a constant dance.

Claire stepped over and looked outside. Amazingly, she now seemed to be on the 1st floor of the building, staring into the courtyard.

A large bonfire roared in the center of the yard, and a series of women danced around the fire, their hair and skin reflecting the bright flames that seemed to orchestrate their movements. There was no music, only wind and fire, and the strange dancing.

The women seemed to be ageless, with long, coarse hair. They wore white T-shirts and ankle length-skirts, their bare feet dirty and constantly moving in a hypnotic, steady rhythm.

Claire found herself mesmerized by the dancing. And in the distance, she could hear a voice whispering in a strange language that made no sense. She knew that standing at the window was wasting valuable time, but she couldn't move. Her energy was gone, and all she could do was stare at the spectacle that defied all logic.

"Are you ready?" Rod stood near the hole, ready to put his leg through it.

Denise nodded, though she was still very unsure. She felt as if the entire evening had turned into a macabre, endless nightmare.

"Ok, here goes."

Denise watched as the deputy maneuvered his body through the hole. She waited for a moment, expecting him to say something, but all she could hear was him grunting as she imagined he was surveying the room around him.

"Here I go," she called out, hoping that she wasn't making a huge mistake.

She put one leg through the hole and then crouched down, pulling her other leg over. The effort was too much, and Denise lost her balance—falling to the ground.

"Ugh. That hurt!" When she looked around, Denise realized why Rod had been relatively silent.

When she'd been married, Denise had enjoyed watching horror movies with her ex-husband, Ben. They kept her entertained way more than romantic comedies or dramas. Her favorite scary flicks were zombie movies, and during better times she'd forced her spouse to sit through them with her.

But never in a million years, would she have imagined that zombies could exist. Not even in her nightmares had they made a special appearance.

Now, however, she and Rod were surrounded by people who couldn't be mistaken for anything else.

There were six of them, standing in a circle—trapping her and Rod in the middle.

Each person was clearly dead. One had an empty eye socket, with dried blood that had pooled around its torn mouth. Another was missing an arm and its right ear, and the others all shared characteristics of the undead.

Worst of all, they were all standing still—just watching them. Not making a sound.

"Holy shit," Denise whispered.

Rod motioned for her to get closer to him.

She took a few steps over to the deputy and noticed that one of the zombies slowly turned to watch her as she changed position.

"What are we going to do?" she whispered, terrified.

"Listen to me very carefully," Rod responded, not turning his head away from the awful creatures around them. "This room has a stairwell. You can't see it right now, because these people are blocking it. But when I first came in here I saw it. Then, these things just ... just appeared."

"We can't just run past them. There's too many. How are we going to get out?" Denise was starting to panic.

Rod turned his head slightly so that he could focus one eye on his companion. "I have a gun. And I plan to use it on these fucking things. When I pull the pistol out of my holster, I need you to run past the one I'm able to take out. Can you do that for me?"

Oh my God. He's going to distract them so that I can get away.

They'll kill him. I can't leave him here. Maybe we can both escape.
As if he could read her thoughts, Rod shook his head. "We can't both run. I can try to get away after I shoot the first one, but one of us has to find your daughter. Look, we don't have much time. I'm not sure how long they're going to stand still."

One of the zombies let out a low moan as if to signal the end of the standoff. The sound reverberated throughout the room, and the other creatures began to shift back and forth.

They were becoming anxious.

Denise felt as if her mind was shutting down. Her body felt frozen in place, every limb stiff and unmoving. The creatures looked like they had stepped right out of a horror movie. They were bloody, rotting and without a soul—their eyes black and wet in the darkness. With very little available light, she could scarcely make out their details, but one thing was for certain—she and Rod were surrounded and it wouldn't be long before they were overtaken by the living dead.

She suddenly felt Rod's hand on her arm. He squeezed her so tightly that she could feel his fingers bearing down on bone and muscle.

"You need to move. Now. Do you understand? I'm going to count to three, and as soon as I do—you run forward. Got it?"

Wincing, Denise nodded.

One of the zombies moaned again and shrugged his shoulders as if to signal that there was no more time left.

"Here we go," Rod whispered, looking around and not demonstrating any emotion.

"One…" he began to reach for his gun.

"Two…" Denise felt sweat dripping down her neck and traveling down her back.

"Three!"

Rod grabbed his gun and began shooting.

The sound was so loud that it broke Denise out of her reverie. She saw a small opening between two zombies—one who appeared to be hit in the head by a flying bullet because it was flailing wildly—and she ran forward.

A hand barely touched her shoulder—but she didn't stop, and ran straight forward in the darkness, her flashlight shining rays on the ground as her body propelled forward, when suddenly, she hit a wall head-on.

The pain was intense as her nose smashed into concrete, and she felt moisture dripping down.

Crap, I probably broke my nose. It hurts like hell.

Turning around wildly, she shone her flashlight back and forth, prepared to fight whatever was coming at her, but there was nothing except darkness behind her.

She turned back to the wall, and shone her flashlight straight ahead. She realized that she had run right into a wall that eventually ended in a countertop.

Her fear turned into shock.

Wait a minute! This is the counter where Lilly and I checked in. How is that possible? I've been running for at least a few minutes. This doesn't make any sense. If I'm at the check-in counter, then Rod shouldn't be far behind me.

Denise turned around and saw him.

Rod was lying on the ground near the front door. He didn't seem to be moving.

The zombies and the maze … were gone.

"Rod!" she shouted, as she ran over to where he lay. "Are you ok?"

As she got closer, it was clear that Rod was definitely *not* ok. He'd been attacked and there was blood pooling next to his neck and arms.

To her horror, Denise could see that something had bitten Rod squarely on the neck and dark fluid was draining out. She quickly put her hand on it as if to stem the flow, and felt panic once again rising up in her throat—threatening to suffocate her entirely.

"Please say something," she managed to whisper, each word stinging the back of her throat.

Rod's lips moved slowly and he mumbled something, too softly for her to hear.

Denise moved closer, and put her ear to his mouth. "What is it?"

"Save her. You can…"

Then he gurgled and stilled. The warm breath that had

emerged from his mouth ... sputtered and ceased.

"No," Denise whispered, pulling back and staring at the deputy. "No, no, no."

18

The dancing women began to flicker, like a dying fire.
Pain in her legs caused Claire to twitch, and she realized that she'd been standing in place for at least several minutes without even realizing it.

Something about what she was watching was so incredibly hypnotic, however. The women were beginning to fade but their movements continued in fluid motion, as if they were marionettes dancing on a carousel that was turning slowly ... methodically.

And then, in a burst of light—they disappeared, leaving Claire in a darkened room once more. And she was once again staring out of a 2nd story window at the darkness, wind and rain beyond.

She felt a twinge in her bladder, and decided that before she resumed her search, she would use the bathroom. Shining her flashlight forward, Claire made her way to the restroom and found the toilet. It seemed clean, so she quickly crouched and urinated. Once she was done, she flushed the toilet, which as she'd hoped, worked. Figuring that the water was on in the building, she walked over to the sink and rested her flashlight on the counter while she washed her hands.

The light from her small flashlight reflected against the wall of the shower. As Claire looked up from the sink, she noticed that the wall was covered in black specks. The curtain was partially drawn, which seemed perfectly normal.

There was a darkness behind them ... which was not...

Claire quickly wiped her hands on her pants, and turned around. Grabbing the flashlight, she turned and pointed it in the direction of the shower. She slowly moved towards it.

There's something behind that curtain. I hope it's not what I think it is.

"Is there someone in there? I'm not going to hurt you. Just come out."

Claire felt pretty ridiculous as she spoke the words but

didn't want to take any chances.

The dark shape on the other side of the curtain didn't move or respond.

Reaching out, Claire pulled the curtain back and gasped.

The dark specks were all over the wall, and inside the bathtub, there was a figure lying flat—splayed out. It looked like one of the deputies because a badge gleamed in the light as Claire's flashlight passed over the corpse's chest.

"It can't be," she whispered.

Almost fearfully, she took a closer look at the face of the dead deputy.

Despite the mangled skin, the nose being essentially crushed and one of the eyelids swollen shut, there was no doubt in Claire's mind who she was looking at.

It was Deputy Javier Cantra.

Holy shit. What happened to him? I have to call for back-up immediately. Or text, or do something. This is way bigger than me. I've got to get out of here and find help. It's time to stop acting like Nancy Drew and let the professionals handle this.

With shaking hands, Claire placed her flashlight between her legs, and reached for the phone in her pocket. She pushed on it, expecting to see it light up, but nothing happened.

"No, no." She pressed buttons and shook the phone, hoping to reach a different conclusion.

The phone remained powerless—the battery clearly drained.

Claire slowly put the phone in her pocket and backed out of the bathroom, finding the bed and sitting down slowly. She tried to collect her thoughts and calm down enough to figure out her next move.

I could jump out of the window. It's pretty high up here. I will definitely sprain something. At least I'll be out of this crazy place. That hallway is endless. I'm never going to find my way out. And the stairwell is gone. How is it possible for something like that to just disappear? No. It's not worth me wandering around for the rest of the night and getting stuck in one of the bedrooms with maniacs from the 1970s. Not sure if they're ghosts or if I'm just imagining things. Either way, I've had enough.

Just then, Claire heard what sounded like chanting. The voices were low and female.

And not very far away at all.

Someone's up here. And it's pretty close! I'd better go at least try to check it out. Maybe they can help me find my way out.

At the same time, a small voice in her mind warned her.

Be careful.

Lilly opened her eyes and looked around.

She was in the hotel room, but everything was bright now and the sun was shining through the window.

Her bed felt soft and clean, and she could smell something that reminded her of the flowers her mother sometimes had in the house.

She sat up slowly and looked around.

The room was sparse, but clean and welcoming. The walls were painted a light yellow and were adorned by a few paintings of different kinds of flowers.

Lilly emerged from the bed and felt very light on her feet. She was wearing a nightgown that was unfamiliar to her. It was white with yellow flowers embroidered on it.

It felt extremely comfortable.

Barefoot, she opened the door and looked out. The door some-how magically opened up to a wide field. Up ahead, a bright blue sky contained a few white puffy clouds and the air was comfort-ably warm with a light breeze. The ground was covered in a soft golden moss. Tiny purple flowers sprinkled the ground in differ-ent spots along the landscape. And in the distance, Lilly could see a smattering of wild oak trees providing shade and respite.

Somewhere in the back of her mind, Lilly knew that the scene before her could not really be happening. She recalled that at some point, she'd been taken back to the inn by a group of women and they'd lain her on a bed in a room upstairs.

But that all seemed very long ago and all that mattered now was here, in this strange, beautiful field.

Lilly knew that her mother was not in this place, but found herself being alright with that fact. She was unafraid and knew that her mother was better off wherever she was … and didn't belong in the field.

She walked along for a short while, when she noticed a woman sitting on the ground not far from her.

The woman was wearing a similar nightgown, only hers was yellow. She had extremely pale skin and full, curly red hair that captured the glow of an unseen sun.

Lilly thought she was absolutely the most beautiful woman she'd ever seen.

Waving at the woman, Lilly caught her attention and felt a surge of happiness when the woman motioned for her to come over.

When Lilly got close enough, she noticed that the woman had the greenest eyes she'd ever seen on a person, and wondered if maybe the woman was a fairy or a princess from a storybook tale.

"Hi," she said shyly. "Do you know where we are?"

The woman laughed, a loud musical sound that frightened Lilly at first because of its intensity.

"Yes, of course, child. This is your happy place. Don't you recognize it?"

Lilly looked around and slowly realized that the scene in front of her was identical to a story that she loved and that her mother had read to her countless times. It was a book about a mouse that found its courage in the fields of gold once it realized that true happiness was something that was created within oneself.

She couldn't remember the name of the book, but she did remember that there was an illustration at the end that had always caught her attention. As a toddler, she'd stare at that picture and wonder what it would be like to run amongst the flowers and golden grass with the talking mice.

"This is from my book," she murmured.

The woman nodded. "Yes, I needed to meet you in a place that you'd find familiar and comforting. Lilly, do you know why you're here?"

Lilly shrugged, "I'm dreaming?"

"Well, yes. You are dreaming, but it's more than that. You're about to change and become a part of our sisterhood. Do you understand what that means?"

Lilly had no idea what the woman was talking about.

"No. I don't have any sisters. My mom only had me and no other kids."

The woman laughed again. "You actually have many sisters, sweet Lilly. These sisters are special and connected to you in a way that is written in the stars. It is a part of the prophecy of our coven. This is something that you must follow, but in order to do so, you will need to be transformed."

"What do you mean?" Lilly asked. It was difficult for her to follow what the woman was saying but something about it was making her nervous.

The woman continued, "In order for you to become like one of us, you must leave your other life behind. Everything that you did in the past, your friends, your home and even your mother … these things, you have to leave behind. We will help you move forward, of course. It is necessary for the full transformation."

"Wait! You mean, I have to leave my mother? I can't leave Mom. She's my mother! You can't take me away from my mother!"

Lilly began backing away and felt panicked. She didn't know what was happening or who the red-headed woman was, she just knew that she had to get away.

Turning, she began to run across the field.

The sky darkened to deep purple, and the ground felt rougher than before. The moss had disappeared into the ground, leaving cracked dirt in its stead.

Lilly's feet hurt from running on the rough ground but she kept on going until she saw the doorway to the room up ahead.

Her breathing labored, and her chest hurting from the exertion, Lilly struggled to reach the doorway.

Just as she was about to step inside, the ground opened up and pulled her in.

Screaming, she fell down into the dark depths of the crater.

As Lilly fought against her transformation and writhed on the bed, squealing in agony—Sephira felt an intense amount of pain slam into her body with full force.

She fell back and snarled, thrashing and screaming at the same time.

Someone had torn open her magic with the power that she could only assume was the bullet from a gun. The attack was so intense that it physically pained her, as if her own body was being torn apart.

She could taste blood in her mouth and spat it out, angrily.

Nyssa rushed to her side while the Elder and other sisters continued their chanting and singing. They were coming upon the most important stage of Lilly's conversion and could not stop, no matter what.

"Are you ok? What happened?" Nyssa asked fearfully. She was not comfortable around Sephira, but they were sisters and she was the only one who wasn't actively engaged in the ceremony. Her main task was to remain by the child's side. So after seeing Sephira literally fly back into the wall, she had no choice but to ensure that the powerful witch was alright.

Sephira winced in pain. There were too many forces at play, draining her energy and weakening her magic. And now, someone had physically torn apart one of her creations, breaking one of her links to the spells she'd created.

Which means those people will be able to get to us. There's still my dark infinity spell that is in place up here, which pulls the paranormal into my loop. But that won't last forever. Both the living and the ghosts take up too much energy and the magic will eventually fade.

Pushing Nyssa aside, Sephira stood up and spoke loudly to be heard over her sister's chanting. "We need to hurry this up. I've done my best to protect us with magic, but there are many other people here now, and they're trying to find us. There's only so much I can do to stop them. It isn't worth it. If she refuses to change, we should get rid of her, and get out of here."

Suddenly, the Elder stopped chanting. She stared at Sephira, then walked up to her and slapped her firmly across the face.

The other sisters continued their chanting but Nyssa just stared at both women in shock.

Sephira felt the sting of the slap against her now quickly withering skin, and fought against the watering of her eyes that threatened to break free.

"You will never say those words again," the Elder said quietly, a coldness behind each word. "This child will join our coven and be one of the most powerful witches in the world. You know the prophecy. We've gone to great lengths to bring her here. We will finish the ritual one way or the other. If you do not want to be a part of this, you know the ramifications. It is your choice. Now, be quiet and do your job. Do not bother us again."

Sephira knew that she could kill the Elder with one flick of her wrist. Her dark magic was very powerful and the Elder was very weak, physically. But she also knew that if she harmed any of her sisters—especially the Elder—she would face the Mother and her fate would be worse than anything imaginable.

The Mother was the all-omnipresent force that guided their coven. She was the beginning and the end—advising them throughout their sisterhood and guiding them on the proper course of action to take. The Mother sometimes appeared through dreams or visions, and could be a guiding light when needed.

She could also teach through discipline and had enforced the ways of the coven for many, many years. There were tales of witches who'd been tortured to death for betraying their coven and yet, they'd never been attacked by any of their sisters. Instead, they'd found themselves facing a horrible end that happened by circumstance—they had died from fire while they slept because their bed burned to the ground due to a fallen candle, their heart had stopped due to a sudden, incredibly painful heart attack and many other 'ends' that had strangely occurred after the betrayal took place.

Sephira didn't doubt for a moment that she would face a similar circumstance if she went entirely rogue. It was what kept her connected to the coven, when all she really wanted to do was escape the sisters and travel throughout the world, wreaking havoc on those who had the misfortune of getting in her way. At times, she feared that she would entirely lose control and just lash out—without thinking of the circumstances.

Nyssa, who remained nearby, wondered privately if Sephira was at the end of her restraint. The witch had lost all the youthful luster she'd put in place and was now simply focusing on keeping her spells active and protective.

Sephira's hair was drab, her face full of wrinkles, and her nose crooked—with a smattering of red veins everywhere.

Nyssa was younger than Sephira and knew that she looked better than her evil sister, which was a disadvantage given current circumstances. She decided that it was best to not make matters worse, and backed away, moving over to the bed where Lilly was now resting once more.

Sephira ignored Nyssa entirely and instead, remained in place by the wall. Her mind churned with anger as she fought to maintain control.

19

Denise sat with Rod's body for a few moments, and periodically wiped at her nose, which burned. She was unsure as to what to do, frightened to be on her own.

She was also incredibly sad. Despite only knowing him a short time, she recognized that the deputy was a good man who'd been trying to help her find Lilly. He'd never given up and because of her predicament, was now … gone.

I can't let his death be in vain. He really tried to help me. I've got to keep going. Otherwise, why did he risk his life? No. I can't just fall apart. I've got to find Lilly. She's in here somewhere. Something is trying to keep me from her, and I won't … I can't let it win.

Denise gingerly reached for Rod's gun and picked it up off the ground where it had fallen—presumably while he'd been attacked by the zombies that had since disappeared. She felt the heavy, cold metal in her hand and wondered if she'd be able to use the firearm if necessary.

Can't think about it right now. Just gotta take it and keep going.

Unsure as to where to put the firearm, she decided to stick the gun underneath her pants and keep it in place by her waistband, which felt tight enough to hold it place.

Standing up, she glanced down at Rod again, feeling a tremendous amount of sorrow and turned around, shining her flashlight around the room.

Once she had her bearings, Denise made her way to the stairwell. She remembered the woman who had checked them in—Bonnie—and wondered if she had even been human. It all felt so distant.

It feels like I have been up for hours. Was she a figment of my imagination? Or was she a part of all that is happening here? There is evil all around me tonight. There is no doubt about that.

Clutching the flashlight, Denise found her way to the stairwell that led upstairs. She took the steps carefully, noticing the candles that lit the way. The candles also seemed surreal, and not entirely in focus.

Nevertheless, Denise did not stop to check them out or get a closer view. She was intent on reaching the second floor.

When she stepped into the hallway, confusion rose in her mind.

The hallway seemed infinite but every few seconds, it would blur and darken.

Denise wiped her eyes, wondering if she was losing her mind.

She took a closer look and could see what looked like a mirage floating just above reality. There was an infinite image that ran on forever, but just underneath, she could see another hallway that ended in a wall.

It was two images juxtaposed on top of each other.

"What kind of dark magic is this?" she asked aloud, not realizing just how close she was to the truth.

Just then, Denise saw a woman exiting one of the rooms, flashlight in hand.

"Hey! Hey!" Denise called out, "Stop! Wait!"

But the woman continued down the hallway and stopped in front of one of the doors at the very end—the darkness making it difficult for Denise to see what was happening.

The exhausted mother did not wait for her flashlight to guide her. She ran forward and prayed that her daughter was nearby.

The singing was louder now, and Claire tried to focus on the sound. It was difficult because the hallway was dark once more and it seemed as if the sounds could be coming from any room.

She forced herself to slow down and listen.

It sounds like women chanting or singing. I've never heard any-thing like this before. It is getting louder now. Wait. I think it is coming from this room.

Claire put her hand on the door to her right, and to her sur-prise, it shifted slightly.

Oh my goodness! The singing is coming from inside that room. Need to get in somehow without anyone seeing me.

The Elder began to sing loudly and moved toward one of the windows in the small room.

She reached out and with very little effort, flung it open without using her hands. She simply focused on a spell inside of her mind and let it flow through her. The magic acted like a river, sweeping through the witch's veins and emerging from her fingertips as it seeped out and wrapped itself around the window.

As the shutters and glass flew open, rain and wind swept through and created chaos.

The Elder felt the stinging pellets of water strike at her arms and legs as the hot wind, specifically generated by tropical storms, raced through her clothing. The heat wrapped itself around her legs and teased her hair into a mess of tangles. It was difficult to see with her eyes, so the Elder focused on seeing with her mind.

The vision of Lilly was clear. The transformation was almost complete. The Elder could feel the Mother permeating the child's spirit and soul, activating what Lilly possessed but did not yet utilize. There was a magical quality to the child that had been gifted at birth, but that had laid dormant until now— the moment of reckoning.

The other sisters continued chanting, but they were exhausted. The room was destroyed, leaves and rain dampening the floors and sending debris everywhere. The storm had picked up considerably and howled, sending a steady stream of rain in every direction.

And in the center, Lilly remained on the bed. She had stopped writhing and moaning, and was now lying in one position, breathing rhythmically.

Nyssa reached down and moved wet strands of hair away from the child's eyes. Lilly's forehead was hot and felt swollen to the touch.

I hope this is over soon. The child is on fire. She will not survive this, if the ritual does not reach its conclusion.

Nyssa vaguely remembered her own transformation. She had been a tormented teenager when the Elder came to her home and snatched her away in the dead of night. At the time, Nyssa was ready. She had been suffering from visions and horrible dreams of dancing straight into burning flames that would melt her skin. Her parents had tried psychiatrists and numerous drugs, before simply giving up on her.

Therefore, when the Elder told her that a transformation would save her from the pain and suffering of her nightmares, Nyssa had been very happy to oblige.

She vaguely remembered the ritual, but knew that the Mother had been there, guiding her into the depths of change. It had not been painless, and at points during the ritual she'd felt as if her mind was going to snap into a million tiny pieces from the strain of the conversion.

When it had ended, Nyssa was different. She no longer felt any attachment to her parents or immediate family members. Sisters and brothers were forgotten, grandparents would no longer be a part of her life and friends—well, she hadn't made any attachments worth mentioning, so that was easy to disregard.

Now, looking down at Lilly who had finally begun to relax, Nyssa felt guilty and sad for those who had loved this child.

She will never be the same again.

At the same time, Nyssa could feel Sephira glaring at her. She knew that the older witch was jealous of the young girl, as she was constantly conjuring up spells to appear beautiful and seductive.

There were stories about Sephira masquerading around town, and bringing men home with her—only to have sex with them and throw them out before her magic faded.

Her magic has definitely faded now. She looks awful. The dark magic she practices doesn't just drain her of energy; it warps her face and mind. She's an absolute monster. And I can feel the hatred emanating from her skin like a poison.

Nyssa continued watching Lilly and felt a strong tug on her heart. For the first time in her life, she felt protective over another human being.

"The ritual is almost over," she murmured. "Lilly, don't worry. We will take care of you."

Claire stared at the scene in front of her. Despite the earlier visions and hallucinations that she knew could not have been real, she had no doubt in her mind that what was happening in front of her wasn't a vision—it was reality.

She looked at the young girl on the bed. To her surprise, even with the wind and rain blowing through, the child was calm. Serene even.

I wonder if they have drugged her. It is impossible to tell if she is alive or dead. Hope I can get her out of here somehow. These women look like the ones I saw dancing in the courtyard. But they can't be the same ones. These people look older.

Just then, another gust of wind swept through and nearly closed the door on Claire.

She pushed back on it and gasped at the same time.

It was enough to draw attention to her presence, and the women all turned to face her. They stopped chanting and glared at her, the rain plastering hair to their faces, glistening moonlight reflected in the droplets that dripped down their cheeks.

"Look, I'm sorry for interrupting. But that child's mother is looking for her. What are you doing?" As the words tumbled from Claire's lips, she felt ridiculous. And she wasn't sure she was safe confronting these strange women. While none of them were obviously wielding any types of weapon, she wondered if there were invisible hidden strengths in the room that could harm her.

One of the women, who looked to Claire like she was one hundred years old, responded in a slow, commanding tone. "You are interrupting our gathering. Give us a few more moments, and we can answer any questions you have."

The other women nodded and murmured to themselves.

"Is the girl ok? I mean, she looks like she's passed out." Claire stumbled, trying to figure out how to keep the conversation going without angering the posse.

"She is fine," the old woman answered. "She has nearly completed her transformation, and will be leaving with us. She's a part of our family. No need for you to worry."

The answer was incredibly dismissive and left Claire feeling powerless to say anything else. But she knew that she couldn't just stand there and allow the child to be harassed or whatever was happening.

Reaching for her gun, she pulled it out quickly and pointed it at the women.

"Hands up!" she shouted. "That child does not belong to you. So just go ahead and stop what you're doing!" Claire then waved the gun from left to right, indicating that they were all a threat.

The women, however, did not move. Instead they simply stood and stared at her.

Claire wondered if the other women were perhaps on drugs or didn't understand English. In all her life, she'd never seen people so unaffected by a gun being pointed at them.

"Why are you just standing there? I told you to move. Get up against the wall."

Once again, the women didn't move—just stared at her with blank faces.

Claire was about to wave the gun around again, when she felt a strange sensation in her legs that traveled down to her feet and all the way to her toes. At first it felt like gentle tickling, but then it grew stronger and began to feel like electrical charges shooting up and down her bones.

"What the hell?" She began looking around and noticed that a particularly grotesque woman behind her was muttering a phrase over and over again while glaring in her direction.

Suddenly, Claire felt her entire body begin to rise above the ground. She tried to twist around again to see what was happening, but now her entire body was being contorted by an unknown force and she found herself lying on her back in mid-air, floating above the ground and rising toward the ceiling. The gun in her hand dropped from her fingers as if coated with gelatin and fell to the ground with a loud thud.

"What's happening?" she shouted.

"First of all, allow me to introduce myself. My sisters know me as The Elder. And you, young lady, are interrupting a very important ritual that we've waited for years to carry out. It has taken us a very long time to be reunited with the chosen one. The child you see has been prophesized to join our coven. And now, she is very close to finishing her transformation. Therefore, we will need to be left uninterrupted as we complete our ceremony. We are almost done."

"No!" Claire shouted. "This isn't right! I don't know who you people are, but you can't do this. This is America, for Christ's sake. You can't just snatch children and take them away from their parents. You must give her back to her mother. Please let me go and stop all of this."

"Let you go?" sneered a voice from behind Claire. "Well, alright if you insist."

And with that, Claire felt a rush of wind as her body fell to the ground, but not before hitting a table on the way down and breaking her neck.

She dropped to the floor in a ruined wreck, her eyes still open and staring at the feet of the woman who'd just ended her life.

"Enough of this!" shouted the Elder. "We've wasted enough time already. Focus. The time is nearly at hand."

Sephira stiffened in irritation. Once again, she'd protected the coven and this was the way her sister repaid her? Where was the appreciation and thanks?

And she hadn't missed the look of disdain on Nyssa's face as the ridiculous, interfering woman with the gun had fallen to her death.

What did she expect? That I would let her live? It is my duty to protect everyone. These are my spells that are keeping the intruders at bay … that is my power. And this is the thanks I get? What would these bitches do if I left the coven and they had to fend for themselves? I've had to work so hard tonight that all of my beauty is gone. Now, everything is old. I'm a fucking hag again.

Anger bubbled up in Sephira's chest. She could feel her heart beating fast, and she clenched her hands into fists, struggling to maintain herself as fury threatened to overtake her.

Denise watched in horror as a gun fell to the ground, followed by a young woman she didn't know—but by the looks of it, she could tell that it was someone who'd worked with Rod.

Her heart lurched at the sight of Lilly lying on the bed.

Her daughter looked peaceful but very pale, and Denise wondered if Lilly had been drugged. Anger threatened to overtake her, and she forced herself to take a deep breath and calm the fury that raced throughout her body.

The women were chanting melodically, but Denise didn't recognize the phrases—and at times it seemed to her as if the women were speaking in another language entirely. The fact that the windows were open and rain and wind continued blowing through didn't make it any easier for her to hear what was being said.

Lilly must be drenched. I've got to get her out of here. I've got to get that gun!

Denise said a quiet prayer and leaning forward, darted toward the gun.

The witches stopped chanting—shocked to see the middle-aged woman lunge across the floor at the gun.

Turning, Denise saw a horribly-aged woman in the corner of the room glare at her. The woman raised her hand as if to point...

Denise didn't hesitate. She pulled the trigger—praying that the safety was off, and felt the shot ring out—reverberating across her body as the sound bounced off the walls around them.

Her aim was dead-on, and the woman she'd been aiming at flew back against the wall and crumbled into a broken heap as the bullet drove a fatal hole through her heart.

As the life left Sephira's body, she weakly tried to hang on—but it was too late. She was magically-powerful, but not immortal.

And as her last breath left her, so did all the spells that she'd been conjuring.

The Countryside Inn shuddered as if feeling a shock of pain and groaned ... its old dusty wood shifting back into place.

The room itself shook and the windows slammed shut in such ferocity that the glass shattered, sending shards in different directions—piercing the witches who stood around Lilly.

They shrieked and fell back, covering their faces—trying to protect themselves from the onslaught.

Denise saw the elderly women recoil and took the opportunity to run to the bed. Without hesitation, she picked up Lilly—who felt surprisingly dry—and carried her out of the room as quickly as she could.

As she ran out of the room, she could hear one of the women calling out, "No! You must leave her with us!"

You've gotta be kidding me. Like hell. We're getting out of here as quickly as humanly possible.

Lilly was heavy, but Denise didn't allow that to slow her down. She vaguely noticed that the hallway was dark and dusty once more, but many of the doors leading to the rooms had blown open and the moonlight shining through the windows helped her navigate to the exit.

The stairwell was easy to find, and Denise carefully maneuvered her body so that she was able to descend the stairs. The candles on the stairwell seemed to be real, because they were still in place and guided her down to the first floor.

Suddenly, there was a loud shriek of anger from the upstairs wing and when Denise burst through the stairwell doorway on to the first floor, she was dismayed to see that she was suddenly surrounded by people dressed for a party.

They were all clothed as if it was the 1950s era and had champagne flutes in their hands.

Music twinkled from a baby grand piano while a man dressed sharply in a tuxedo, played Beethoven's piano sonata no. 8, Pathetique.

Lilly stirred in her arms and moaned—the sounds beginning to wake her.

"Shhh," Denise whispered. "Go back to sleep. We are getting out of here."

With as much care as possible, Denise began to wind her way around the partygoers, trying not to look at any of them in the eye.

She had made it past several couples when a cold hand pressed itself against her arm, causing Denise to jump up in shock.

"Oh, I'm sorry, honey," a pale faced woman with short black hair purred. She was beautiful but very pale, and her lips were ruby red. "Didn't mean to scare you. Just wanted to tell you what a sweet little girl you have."

Denise wasn't sure how to answer her, but decide that being polite would be a better course of action.

These creatures or hallucinations or whatever they are can be fickle. Don't want to piss her off. Not with Lilly in my arms.

Smiling, Denise tried to be as genuine as possible. "Why, thank you. That is very nice of you to say."

The woman looked down at Lilly, and reached at, caressing the child with her finger.

Lilly twitched at the touch, and Denise figured it was because the woman's hands were very cold. Trying to be subtle, she backed away slightly and smiled again.

"I'm sorry we can't stay and chat. It's very late and we should be heading home."

The woman scrunched up her nose in confusion. "But you can't leave. The party's just getting started. And you don't have the keys."

Then, the woman turned away and began speaking with another partygoer.

Denise stood in place for a moment and then realized that she was indeed missing her car keys. They were still upstairs in her room.

Where those crazy old women are. Oh shit. What am I going to do now?

The Elder was furious. Not only had they been interrupted twice, but with Sephira now dead, the spells she'd fabricated had been broken, which would allow the woman and child to easily flee the building.

Her sisters were also clearly shaken, slowly rising to their feet and looking at each other with shocked expressions on their faces.

"What do we do now?" Nyssa quietly asked.

"The metamorphosis was nearly complete. We must slow their departure so that we have time to catch them. At that point, it is really up to Lilly. She should know her destiny. It is never entirely certain, however. Let's join hands now and conjure up a spell to delay their escape."

The elderly women moved closer to each other. They formed a circle and clasped each other's hands and once that was complete, they began murmuring the prayer of the fragmented.

It was a prayer that pulled from memories and fears, creating a nightmare, woven into a tapestry of former frightening experiences.

The Elder was concerned that the prayer wouldn't be strong enough. She knew that Sephira was really the only one who had dabbled in truly powerful, dark magic.

But she is at peace now. That is best. Her tortured soul will rest for eternity. The Mother works in mysterious ways.

As they chanted in unison, the Elder wondered if the Mother had abandoned Sephira in her last moments. The secrets of life and death were reserved for those existing in those respective states and only the dead could truly understand death. She hoped that the Mother would be merciful on Lilly and on her coven—allowing them to complete the ritual and retreat back to their peaceful existence in the woods where their cabins— deeply hidden amongst the foliage, would continue to provide them with refuge.

Before that could happen however, she needed to focus on the prayers at hand.

Closing her eyes, she sang aloud:

Let the colorful thoughts of memories past,
Strike true and true in the days of present,
The sting of the touch is not mean to last,
It will just surround its people whilst we lament.

20

5:00 AM

Denise stood for a moment, feeling Lilly shift in her arms again. She looked around the room at the partygoers and to her horror, she realized that the man playing the piano was a zombie.

He had turned and was looking at her, a gruesome smile on his ruined face. Half of his mouth was torn away, and his sunken eyes were black pits fixated in her direction.

In the corner of the room, a woman was straddling a man on the couch. She was stabbing him repeatedly in the throat with a knife as he simply stared up at her with sadness in his eyes.

Denise wasn't sure when the scene had begun to change into a macabre series of mini-events, but it was enough to break her reverie and make the decision for her.

Fuck the car keys. We're getting out of here.

Taking a deep breath, Denise began walking purposefully toward the door. She was fully anticipating that someone would grab her if she tried to run.

Here we go. Step by step. Just need to sidestep this drunken guy who is spilling his drink on the ground. Ok, keep going straight. Don't let anyone stop you. Keep moving. Keep moving.

A woman reached out toward her, as if to grab her arm, but Denise was ready and quickly moved out of the way.

Reaching out, Denise grasped the door handle and twisted, pushing it outward.

As soon as the door opened, a gust of wind and rain swept through, nearly taking her breath away.

Just then, Lilly opened her eyes.

"Mommy?"

Without looking in her child's direction, Denise answered, "We're leaving."

And with that, she raced out of the building and into the parking lot.

There was a shriek and a loud bang behind her, but Denise didn't look back—instead she tried to maneuver around the cars that were parked in front of the structure and ran into the street. It was extremely difficult, because Lilly felt like a sack of rocks, so once she made it into the road, Denise stopped and tried to catch her breath.

Wind and rain were constant now, coming down in waves and streaming down her face—making it nearly impossible to see.

"Lilly. Can you walk?"

The child was now looking at her with a terrified look on her face. But she nodded quickly.

"I think so."

Denise put her down gently and watched as Lilly struggled to get to her feet.

"Are you ok?" Denise asked, "Do you remember anything? I was so worried."

Lilly rubbed her eyes and looked around. "Where are we? All I remember is this place. And there were flowers, and this woman who told me that I belonged to something very special. I feel … different."

Denise shook her head impatiently. "Ok, there's really no time for this. We've got to get out of here. You were kidnapped by these crazy women. We don't have any choice. Let's try to get to town where we can get some help. My purse and all of my things are still up in the room."

Lilly didn't say anything and simply followed her mother as they walked quickly along the road. The storm continued around them, wind and rain hitting them from all different directions.

Given the cloud cover, it was still dark around them, but Denise knew that sunrise would eventually come, and she welcomed the thought. It gave her hope.

Until she saw the line of women up ahead, blocking their way.

21

They were a strange bunch. Six women standing in a line, calmly staring straight ahead.

Each individual witch was elderly, some extremely aged—while others were in their late fifties or early sixties.

They all wore long dresses that were drab and gray, hanging on their bodies like limp rags. The garments were large and hung loose, removing any sense of shape or style.

In the center, a woman with long white hair looked at Denise and Lilly. Somehow, she—with the others—had simply appeared in the center of the road. And yet, the woman was neither breathing heavy nor fatigued—despite the fact that everyone had been up all night long.

Something about her cold confidence frightened Denise. It was as if she had a job to do and nothing more.

And her job was to claim Lilly for her own.

No fucking way.

Denise moved in front of Lilly, blocking her daughter from the witches.

"What do you want?" she yelled, trying to be heard over the wind.

"I am the Elder. And these are my sisters." The woman with the long white hair spoke slowly and somehow, her voice was strong—carrying over the constant howling of wind.

"What do you want?" Denise repeated.

"She wants me," Lilly said quietly from behind her mother.

Denise twisted around and stared at her daughter.

Lilly looked very small at that moment, but she wasn't shivering or frightened. Instead, she was calm—her eyes large and unwavering. Wisps of brown hair clung to her forehead, wet from the rain.

She looks angelic, but suddenly, Denise was very afraid.

"She can want whatever she wants. It doesn't matter. You're going home with me. These women are crazy." Reaching for her daughter's hand, Denise began to pull her in the other direction.

Lilly however, refused to budge.

"What's wrong? We need to get away from them right now!" Denise could hear the wavering of her own voice, and choked back on the saliva that was gathering in her mouth.

"No, mom. I can't go with you."

The words stung like sharp daggers, stabbing her in every possible area of exposed flesh. The idea that her daughter wouldn't … or couldn't … come with her, simply wasn't a reality that she would accept.

Not letting go of Lilly's hand, Denise pulled her closer.

"What do you mean? We have to go. Right. Now." Denise felt the words fall from her lips as she spit them out. Anger and fear comingled in her mind—but she refused to let the reality of what was happening seep into her consciousness.

"Mom." Lilly held up one hand. "Stop."

Denise felt her strength evaporate and released her grip. "What, Lilly? What's going on with you? Why aren't you listening to me?"

Lilly's eyes never left her mother' face.

"I can't explain it, but things are different now. Something happened to me tonight, and I'm not the same. Those women standing there, they are a part of me now. We are connected by a large force who has found all of us. We are meant to be a part of the sisterhood."

Denise shook her head, "This is ridiculous. You've been brainwashed. Stop all of this talk, and let's go."

But Lilly shook her head and instead, stared sadly at her mother—a tear dripping down her cheek.

And at that moment, right before her eyes, Lilly disappeared from view.

Denise swung around and once again, looked at the line of women standing at the other side of the road.

Lilly stood between them and despite the distance, Denise could her daughter's voice as she shouted out.

"Goodbye, Mom. I'll always love you. Goodbye!"

The women on either side of Lilly turned to face her and as they did, their figures grew faint and they disappeared from view.

22

For Denise, the next few days were a whirlwind of activity, despair and disappointment.

State law enforcement stepped in, trying to understand the murder and mayhem that had descended upon the small city. The dead were taken away, and the Countryside Inn was shuttered for good—its doors sealed, its windows boarded up.

Denise was questioned for hours by investigators. She felt like the disappearance of her daughter was merely one additional technicality that the police were considering. They had so many victims, after all.

There was talk of witches and crazy women who practiced black magic, but deep inside, Denise knew that no one believed her story. She felt crazy even trying to recap it all.

And after weeks of searching—there was no point. There was nothing to find.

Denise knew in her heart that her daughter was gone.

She returned to Miami in tears, her heart empty ... her mind unable to process reality.

23

Forty Years Later

Pain was such a part of normalcy that Denise barely felt like complaining.

The cancer had done ... what cancer does. It found ways to pollute her body, by simply being itself and reproducing—everywhere.

She hadn't noticed the aches and pains until it was too late.

Several months back, the doctor had conducted his many tests, poking and prodding her with needles ... and when it was all done, he'd looked at her with a maddening sympathy reflected in his eyes.

"You have breast cancer. It has spread to the lymph nodes and to your lungs. That's why you've been so tired and short of breath lately. We believe it may also be in your brain. I'm so sorry to have to share this news."

The words stung, but Denise had gotten used to pain and disappointment. After Lilly's disappearance, it was as if part of her had disappeared as well.

The pain of losing her daughter, and the searches that she'd carried out, had consumed most of her life. Denise spent months on the road, trying to uncover anything about the witches she'd seen on that fateful night, but she was met with resistance, disbelief and oddly enough, fear.

They know something. That's why they dismissed me and my questions. They just didn't want to get involved in what happened to my daughter. It's not that they didn't care. They're just frightened.

Friends had come around, trying to make her feel better—but Denise had shunned them all, sinking deeper and deeper into a depression.

Eventually she'd found solace in a local library, taking a part-time job and losing herself amongst the stacks. It was better to immerse herself in the stories of others than try to handle what her life had become and the large hole in her heart.

She thought of Lilly every day.

The monitor in her living room suddenly make a loud "blipping" sound, meaning that her blood pressure had changed.

Denise wasn't surprised. Whenever she thought of Lilly, she got agitated. Even now ... forty years later.

Her diagnosis was grim. She'd self-sustained as long as possible, but the pain was now too intense. She was under hospice care—paid for by her ex-husband's children who felt badly for her and were extraordinarily generous. The only good thing Ben had ever done for her.

A nurse tended to her needs every day, while she lay on a small bed and waited to die.

Denise knew that time was drawing near. It was growing harder and harder to focus, and the intense pain was now numbed by the constant morphine drip that provided sickly sweet solace in her final hours.

"Miss, I'll be right back," the nurse said as she shuffled off in the direction of the bathroom.

Denise weakly raised her hand as if to say, "Sure, alright. Leave me here in my misery."

She liked the nurse, a stout African-American woman named Latonda. The nurse was kind and gentle, with a knack for dealing with someone who was facing their mortality.

Denise felt a stab of pain in her chest. It was searing and cut deep.

I guess this is it, she thought and began to close her eyes.

Suddenly, she felt a gust of wind pass through the room. At the same time, she smelled an odd scent—like the faintest smells of burning incense.

A wooden, floral smell.

Denise opened her eyes and let out a small gasp...

Standing over her hospital bed was a woman in her early fifties. She had streaks of gray in her hair and wore a simple blue peasant dress. Her skin was wrinkled, but Denise saw a flash of energy behind the chocolate brown eyes.

Denise was sick and dying, but she knew her daughter's face. It was an older visage to be sure ... and maybe slightly different.

But it was still Lilly.

"Hush, mom. Don't say a word. It's your time. I'm sorry that I haven't been able to visit all of these many years. I wanted you to know that I'm ok. I'm safe. And I've come to escort you back to your next life."

Denise felt another searing stab in her heart and wondered if Latonda was nearby.

The world grew hazy and it was hard to focus.

With a gasping breath, Denise reached out and clutched her daughter's hand, a tear forming in the corner of her eye.

Latonda Williams was feeling sick. The seafood she'd eaten the night before definitely wasn't agreeing with her.

After flushing the toilet, she went to the sink to wash her hands—staring at her reflection in the mirror.

I look like shit. But it's best to not complain. That poor woman in the living room doesn't have much time left, and I never hear her complaining. Bless her heart. She just seems so sad all the time. It would've been nice for her to just have a little piece of happiness before departing this world.

Latonda stepped out into the living room and was about to ask Denise if she needed anything, when all the air left her lungs. She stood in shock, not believing her eyes.

The hospital bed was no longer occupied … other than a few twigs and leaves that were piled neatly in the center of the blankets.

And the smell of pine and incense filled the air.

Famine

It started with death.

But the dying creature was so small that no one noticed. No one wept, no one panicked, and no one realized that the death of the tiny flea would be the beginning of the end of the world.

The tiny insect felt its small innards begin to twist and ache. It didn't quite understand why its little legs were becoming immobile. The bug's ability to leap from one spot to the other was eliminated as the virus quickly overtook its immune system … destroying it in minutes.

Finally, completely exhausted and unable to stand on all fours, the flea struggled and toppled over on its back.

Moments later, bugs all over the world began to experience the same fate. The "insect killer" as the media called it, was a phenomenon unknown to scientists and entomologists. It was a virus that only affected insects, but was able to kill them rapidly and without any mercy.

So much for the philosophy that cockroaches would inherit the earth upon a nuclear disaster. They died in droves, their bodies littering streets, homes, and sidewalks as the virus took its toll and found its victims.

At first, the uneducated and easy-to-please were thrilled. No bugs meant no mosquito bites, annoying infestations, and even better, no Nile viruses or bug-related transmitted diseases to worry about.

While the initial disappearance of most of the insects on the planet made many phobic people happier than clams, entomologists warned that it was the beginning of a global disaster.

Because without the bugs, birds and other wildlife that included insects in their diet would be severely impacted. No one was quite sure how bad it would get, but many different philosophies prevailed.

In the end, it was worse than anyone had anticipated.

Initially, the anteaters and other mammals that had diets solely dependent on insects were the first to perish. But then, the birds began to die, followed by reptiles, and then larger creatures disappeared as their lifeless bodies sank to the ground. The circle of life that began with the smallest of hearts had been broken and nature's ecosystem was fast to disintegrate.

The flora so dependent on pollination started to wilt and the entire face of the planet changed and grew brown with death.

Scientists tried to fight the degradation and began to "grow" insects in their laboratories, setting them free to multiply and reproduce. The idea that insects could not spread in mass was difficult to grasp since historically they'd been eradicated only through the most powerful of poisonous powders and sprays.

But now, it was different. For as soon as the tiny creatures wriggled their way out of the laboratories and into the common air of the world, they were stricken by the same virus as their predecessors and fell to their deaths within minutes of feeling the first winds of freedom against their wings.

The issue of food also began to grow like a pain that spreads until it's impossible to remember where or when it began.

At first, the news reported high prices for beef, chicken and fish. Then, the prices became so high that most ordinary citizens couldn't afford to buy genuine beef or poultry and had to settle for secondary meats. The soy industry soared as manufacturers created "faux chicken" and other meals made solely from soy and flavorings.

That lasted for a few years, but by then, the famine had hit. Entire species disappeared from the planet and the dietary woes of the world began to create panic. People started to hoard food in their homes, and grocery stores became violent places.

Security guards and then police were hired to stand guard outside the stores to ensure that people followed the rationing rules and didn't fight with each other or try to steal from the grocers. The government was forced to step in and provide assistance in neighborhoods where crime was regularly reported. But it didn't matter ... the crooks found ways to infiltrate even the nicest of neighborhoods.

People were starting to get hungry.

It was a strange sensation, and one that initially only the poorest had experienced. But no longer. Famine had found its way into the middle class.

And that is where my story begins...

You see, my family was a normal, middle class clan made up of two children and two married parents. We lived in a modest home, and with both my parents employed as teachers, we had a generally good lifestyle before the famine.

But once it hit, we felt the high price of food and as the situation grew worse and worse, my parents had a difficult time preserving our once-idyllic childhood.

Meals became strained as my mother struggled to find things for us to eat. She spent hours in lines, waiting for the meals the government was now helping to fund. But the packaged feasts consisted of strange concoctions, chemicals and processed foodstuffs that were no more natural than the table they were being served on.

In essence, the vitamin industry was keeping people from becoming completely nutrient deprived, but it didn't matter. The levels of sickness were rising and the death toll from starvation and malnutrition was now a growing threat.

My mother was the first to succumb to illness and died within three months of kidney failure. Then, my sister passed away. It left my family ruined, and my father with only one person he could rely on.

Me.

Even at a mere 15-years-old, I knew that time was running out. I'm not sure exactly when the fragility of mortality struck me, but certainly seeing my mother and sister die of illnesses related to malnutrition was enough to permanently scar my innocent mind.

There were other things too.

I could see the bones in my body. Having always been

slightly overweight, there were curves and lines that had been hidden from me most of my life. Now however, when looking in the mirror, I could see my collarbone sticking out in rigid defiance.

My ribs were also clearly visible, even when I exhaled, giving my stomach a strange bloated appearance.

And of course, I was hungry constantly. It made everything at home appear edible.

School was a thing of the past, with people starving and struggling to stay alive. So, I had loads of time to roam my house, staring at objects that weren't able to satisfy my appetite. Some days I was so hungry that I tried to eat things like my shirt, hoping the cotton would expand in my stomach and ease the gnawing pain. But that only served to make me sick and send me racing to the bathroom.

My father tried to feed us something for breakfast, lunch and dinner. We ate tiny portions of processed foods that were stale or tasteless or downright terrible. But it was at least … something.

Things were getting worse, and the looting and crime outside were becoming so violent that in a final attempt to control the situation from becoming complete anarchy, the government ordered everyone to stay home until further notice or face absolute death.

It wasn't an empty threat.

The first day of the quarantine, I could hear gunshots ring out as people ignored the warnings and ventured outside. From my window, I could see bodies tumble to the ground in unnatural heaps of death.

"Don't look at that, son," my father ordered. "Let's go down to the basement and stay there for awhile. It's the safest place for us right now."

Together, we loaded up all the remaining cans and bags of food from the kitchen and began the trek downstairs. Our basement was a narrow room underneath the house that was only accessible by a long staircase. The entranceway was sealed by a trap door that could be locked from the inside in the event of disaster.

"You go down first," my father instructed. "Make sure you watch where you're going. These stairs are getting old. I'll come down once I'm sure the house is secure."

More gunfire rang out from the street and the sounds of screaming could be heard. It sounded like a woman going mad. My father's face became increasingly stern.

"Come on, boy. Let's get moving."

As carefully as I was able, I descended the stairwell, trying not to lose my balance. As I stepped on the fifth stair down, I could feel the wood crunch underneath my foot. It felt soft and weak. Quickly, I eased my weight off the wood and moved down to the next step. Finally, my feet connected with the concrete and I was on ground level.

"One minute," my father called out. And then I could hear his footsteps racing overhead as he checked the house. I could almost imagine horses galloping upstairs as my father's shoes made telltale clanking sounds against the wooden floors.

Suddenly, there was a loud crash. I jumped and looked up uncertainly. My father shouted something and then appeared at the basement entrance. Instead of carrying his sack of food downstairs, he quickly tossed it towards me and it landed at my feet, cans and bottles rolling everywhere. Some of them were now broken, spilling their contents along the floor.

Why did he do that? I wondered.

My father began to quickly descend the stairs, when there was a loud *crack.*

The fifth stair collapsed and my father stumbled. For a moment I watched him in slow motion, waving his arms and trying to regain his balance. In a sickening display of approaching disaster, his entire body swayed and fell backward as he tumbled down the stairs.

I could now hear strange noises upstairs and my mind screamed at me to do something, so I raced up the stairwell (mindful to step over the broken stair) and quickly pulled down the trapdoor, locking it into place. It was made of concrete and thudded as it landed flat.

As soon as I knew the door was locked and secure, I raced down to check on my father who was moaning as he lay on the floor. His body was in a strange position, with his legs bent at unnatural angles. Blood dripped from a cut along his head and his eyes were closed.

Suddenly, someone banged on the trapdoor. I stood silent, fear coursing through my veins and escaped urine trickling down my pant leg. I'd never been so scared in my life.

"Open the fucking door!" someone shouted on the other side.

I remained silent.

The invader screamed again and tried to wiggle and kick the door, but the concrete slab remained firmly closed. I recalled that my father had once told me that an engineer had designed the door for a tornado or major disaster and that it was breach-proof.

It seemed like an hour, but the threatening and screaming finally stopped. Everything went quiet and I was finally able to check on my father. A series of light bulbs hung from the ceiling and were operated by the electricity from the house. Thankfully they were still on, which meant that the power hadn't been cut off.

Kneeling down beside my father, I took a nearby rag and gently wiped the blood from his face.

"Dad," I whispered. "Are you ok?"

He moaned in response. I decided to let him rest, and opened up a can of faux sardines, placing them on a few stale crackers.

That was my dinner. And I drank some water before finally shutting off the lights in the basement. We had a small, walled off toilet in the corner that was a modest luxury. I urinated and returned to my father, covering him with a blanket. Then, I took another blanket and fell asleep nearby.

The next day, my father woke me up with his moaning. I rose from the floor and went over to check on him. He had urinated on himself and the smell of piss was strong and acrid. In addition, his face was taking on a strange color of blue.

"Dad," I said, trying to revive him. "Dad, you had a really bad fall. Are you ok?"

He opened his eyes and stared at me as if he didn't know who I was. Then, he closed his eyes again.

The rest of the day was slow and stressful. There were still noises upstairs and every once in awhile I would hear the galloping on the ceiling above my head. But no one tried banging on the door again, which was a small relief.

As nighttime approached (I was able to gauge via my watch), my father's breathing began to worsen and became more labored. I tried to get him to drink something, but he was completely immobile and the liquid simply dripped down his lips. He also urinated on himself again and it was upsetting to see him in such an awful state.

Having barely eaten anything all day, I allowed myself a small piece of stale, moldy bread and a tiny chunk of soy cheese. It didn't do much to calm the aching in my stomach, but I told myself that in a few days things would get better.

I cried myself to sleep that night.

I awoke to the sound of gunfire.

It was coming from above me and there were people screaming. The sounds of glass breaking and things crashing to the ground reverberated from every direction. I cried and shouted for it to stop, but no one listened to me. The clamoring went on and on, until finally there was one extremely loud *thud* and all went quiet.

My father hadn't reacted to any of the noise and remained still on the ground. As I crawled up to check on him, my hand connected with his arm.

He was ice-cold.

"No, no, no," I muttered and checked my father's chest for a heartbeat. There was nothing thudding and his chest felt hollow and cold.

He was dead. I was alone.

Backing away from my father's lifeless body, I ran up the stairs.

I've got to get help. Someone will see what's going on and help me. I've got to get out of here.

Once I reached the top of the stairs, I placed my hands against the concrete slab and with some effort, was able to slide the metal latch away and out of position. Then, I placed my hands on the smooth surface of the door and pushed upward, expecting the slab to easily prop open.

It wouldn't budge.

Bile rose in my throat and panic began to make my vision blurry. But, I bit it down as much as possible and tried again and again to push the door open.

No matter what I tried, it wouldn't shift. Not even an inch.

I was trapped in the basement with my dead father.

The rest of the day was a blur, as I was unable to control my fear. Tears poured down my face as I rocked back and forth and watched my father's lifeless body.

This isn't fair. I shouldn't be down here. I should be upstairs, in the clean, fresh air. I want my mom and sister. But now, they're gone and Dad's gone too. I'm all alone.

It was a difficult concept for my 15-year-old mind to grasp. And it got to the point where the reality was so impossible to accept that my mind shut down. All I wanted to do was sleep.

So, I did.

A month had passed and I'd completely run out of food.

Trying to keep the basement as clean as possible, I'd sorted out neat piles and carefully wrapped everything to keep the smell of rot at a minimum.

I was now drinking water from the toilet, because all of my bottled water was gone. Thankfully, the toilet still flushed, though I wasn't sure what condition my house was in.

A few days after his death, I dragged my father's body to one of the furthest corners of the basement and wrapped his stiffening form in several blankets. It helped to hide his corpse, but it didn't eradicate the onset of rigor mortis and as his body began to decay, the sweet smell of rotting flesh invaded the stale air in rolling waves.

There was one vent in the basement, but I hadn't felt any cool breezes in days and now lived under a constant sheen of sweat that covered my face and arms. It was an uncomfortable feeling but not nearly as uncomfortable as the hunger that was threatening to overtake me.

I was starving to death.

After a few days of no food, my mind began to drift and rationalize the unthinkable. It was as if another person was now talking to me and trying to get me to take steps that were the most horrible I'd ever considered.

There's meat down here, the voice carefully explained to me. *It's not the best quality in the world, but you've got to eat. It'll be like chicken. Just cut off a small piece. If it doesn't taste good, what's there to lose?*

The voice continued in my head for a full day more, and by the fourth day of no food, I could barely walk. If I didn't eat something soon, I'd fall asleep and never wake up. There was already a constant pounding in my forehead and it was a struggle to focus on anything but the voice.

Eat. You must eat. There's no choice.

Do it.

With a stifled sob, I crawled over to where my parents had put the box cutter. I remembered how excited my father had been to buy it on sale and how my sister and I had watched him comically open boxes while making sounds like the legendary karate master, Bruce Lee. We'd laughed and laughed that day.

It all seemed like a different world now.

Carefully picking up the box cutter, I held it in my hands and pushed the button that released a sharp, gleaming blade. I wondered how long it would take for me to die if I pushed it into my heart.

Eat.

The voice was louder now, insistent and urgent. Turning to my father, I crawled over to where he laid wrapped in a blankets, smelling the strengthening fumes of rot. Lifting the bottom of a blanket that covered his legs, I saw how mottled and pale his calf had become.

Do it.

Taking a deep breath, I shoved the blade into my father's leg and silently shrieking, sliced a portion of skin away from the bone. Given that the body was already rotting, the skin and muscle actually tore away easily, allowing me to strip it off in one quick swipe.

Surprisingly, there wasn't a lot of blood. But as I held the meat and skin in my hand, my eyes fluttered and my entire brain threatened to shut down. The world swayed back and forth like a ship at sea, and finally everything settled back.

It was now or never.

I closed my eyes and shoved the lumpy mass into my mouth, not even trying to chew it and did my best to swallow as much as possible. Bile rose in my throat and for a moment I was certain that everything was going to come back up in a wave of vomit.

But somehow, miraculously, it all stayed down.

Taking a deep breath, I looked at my father's leg, now sliced open and shining. My body suddenly began to shake and desire … more.

I pushed the blanket up further and sliced again, finding more soft meat and muscle and once again, shoved it into my mouth so that I couldn't taste anything. Pure sustenance was the objective now and nothing else mattered.

It took nearly an hour, but after swallowing a large portion of the skin and muscle off my father's right leg, my appetite was finally sated.

Carefully covering my father's leg with the blanket, I crawled away and sobbed until exhaustion overtook me.

I ate a little portion of my father every day after that.

His legs went first, and then I started on his torso, and finally worked my way up each arm. Eating had become an obsession and despite my initial horror at the fact that I'd resorted to cannibalism, all reason had been swept away by the simple desire to live.

To complicate matters, I was also starting to feel terribly sick. Something was wrong, but with no way out and no possible access to a doctor, I was forced to ignore the pain in my stomach and the increasing nausea that wracked my body at different times throughout the day.

When the vomiting began, I knew that things weren't good.

At first, I threw up a little and was able to force the rest back down, drinking water and resting my head against the wall.

But then, the vomiting came back and became more violent and in these new fits of sickness, I was losing my entire precious meal down the toilet.

Each time I threw up, I'd wait an hour or so and then eat another slice off my father's frame. But it seemed to make things worse and I'd be back vomiting at the toilet once again.

This continued until I finally curled up in a little ball and went to sleep without even taking the time to cover my father's mutilated corpse.

I woke up the next day shivering and covered in sweat. For the first time in nearly five years, I didn't want to eat anything. My stomach felt raw and lined with thorns.

So I went back to sleep and awoke only to vomit or use the bathroom.

My father's body remained uncovered and rotting.

The next day arrived and with it … the realization that I was going to die.

For starters, I couldn't eat anything at all. My body had completely decided to reject all food. It also wouldn't allow me to drink anything, because when I did, the liquid returned to the surface with such ferocity that it physically hurt.

I was also vomiting up blood and choking every time the spasms hit. A raging fever was traveling through my body and there was nothing left to fight it. My immunity was gone and my will to live had disappeared with the last swallow of my father's flesh.

Time was coming to an end.

As I lay on the ground underneath a heavy blanket, I thought about my family. We'd never been an extremely religious group, but had visited church during the holiest of holidays and I was clear on what was described as "The Kingdom of Heaven." In my feverish mind, I imagined that Heaven would be a place where there was no pain, no suffering, and most of all, no hunger. I looked forward to seeing my mother, father, and sister and wondered if they were watching … waiting for me to join them.

The rest of the day rolled along as my body began to shut

down. I no longer felt the need to urinate and wondered if perhaps my kidneys had failed me. There was a dull pain in my back and every so often, I'd have a sharp pain in my chest that radiated throughout my shoulders and down my arms.

It seemed like numerous ailments were fighting over who would have the chance to finally finish me off.

It turned out that none of them would get the chance to send a final blow while I was alert, because merciful sleep decided to take me from the cruel world that I'd been left in. But before my eyes closed for the last time, I noticed that my father's body seemed to be moving.

At first, I figured it was because I was dying and my mind was playing awful tricks on me. But, as I stared harder at my father's body, I realized that there were maggots wriggling around in his flesh and a small fly was crawling around the half eaten muscles lining his arms.

It was then, right before my death that the horrible realization set in. It was almost funny, and had I been able to laugh, it would have been a hearty sound. But in my dying state, I was only able to give a partial grin at the thought that somehow in my tiny prison, insects had found their way back to the world.

I watched as the fly left my father's body and made its way towards the air vent.

Good luck, I thought as my eyes closed for the final time.

The little fly turned as if to look at me, and then disappeared within the slats of the vent. It flew through the shaft and emerged outside, where other flies were happily feasting on the bodies that had been purposefully left to rot on the hot asphalt.

The circle of life was once again ready to begin.

Stairwell

It never looks right.

It never smells quite right, either.

The stairwell is the most obvious and effective way for me to escape at the end of a long workday. All I have to do is quickly make my way down a short hallway lined with cubicles and then push on a metal bar, which, in turn, opens the heavy stairwell door.

Being on the second floor means that I don't have to descend many flights of stairs, so that's good, but there's still something that happens once the door slams shut, leaving me alone in the musky-smelling dimness.

It scares me.

Not something a forty-five-year-old man wants to tell his wife of nearly a decade.

"Hey, honey, how was your day?"

"Oh, it was great. Finished a ton of budgeting Excel spreadsheets and nearly took a shit in my pants when I had to leave."

"Oh? Why's that?"

"I'm kinda scared of the stairwell. It's dark and smells funny. Sometimes I hear weird creaking noises."

"That's nice, dear. Can you set the table for supper?"

I know the conversation wouldn't go like that exactly, but my wife and I have entered into a hazy state of affairs that keeps our marriage on automatic. It's as if we have to conserve power so that we operate on just enough energy to stay alive for as long as we can.

Needless to say, I can't tell her about my fears. I've just got to face them.

And there's something just not right about that stairwell.

It's dark and smells like chlorine, and despite having fluorescent lights everywhere, it seems *green*. Everything is dirty but that's not the worst part.

At first, it seems like just a dank, horrible stairwell, but as you make your way down the stairs, it feels as if there's something watching you. And not in the embarrassing sense either. It feels like someone is standing right behind you, waiting to grab your wrist and spin you around.

After that, I can only suspect that being pushed and experiencing a painful injury or death might be in order.

But it's all crazy, right?

It's just a normal fucking stairwell.

So I've decided to go back to work tonight and sit in that damned stairwell for at least one hour. Or as long as it takes me to get over this ridiculous paranoia.

Ok, I'm here.

The office is really quiet and dark. It smells like—I don't know—some kind of carpet cleaner. Everything feels sterile. I wonder if the energy people exude is really palpable to the point where it actually warms the air and makes it more bearable because everything just feels cold. And empty.

Maybe I'm just scared.

There it is. The door to the stairwell. When it's closed, it seems very innocent and it really fits the décor in here. It's painted a dull shade of yellow, just like the rest of the office. So if you didn't look closely, you'd think it was just part of the wall.

Buzz, buzz.

Ok, phone's vibrating in my pocket. Let's see who it is.

Don't forget to pick up the milk on your way home. Thanks.

Ah, the wife. She thinks that I'm out visiting my buddy Drake. I told her we were going to have a beer and discuss his divorce.

It's kind of sad, because Drake is a good friend and I really should be there for him. But this stairwell matter is much more important.

And now I have to buy milk on my way back. Good thing I only plan on being here for an hour or two.

Time to open this door.

One…

Two…

Three…

Push!

Screeeech.

Have I mentioned how annoying that sound is? Not just because it is like nails on a chalkboard, but more so because it draws attention to the fact that you are escaping your work-like prison. So, once you push on the metal bar, you typically have to make a very fast getaway or you'll get that subtle-yet-disapproving look from the asshole nearby like, "Why do you get to leave early, while I have to slave away in this cubicle?"

This time, however, I'm not feeling the need to rush things. Rather, I'm going to take it slow because even though the stairway's lit (a huge relief, because I wasn't quite sure whether that's the case after hours), it's still dank and, frankly, horrible.

So, I'm taking my time.

Slam!

Ok, now I'm inside, and I already feel nervous. It smells so bad in here. I can't tell if it's a mixture of chlorine and sweat or just fumes from the other office spaces permeating the vents. It's kind of warm as well, so I'm not sure if there's even any air-conditioning on in here at all.

Just the thought is making me feel claustrophobic.

Ok, ok. I need to calm down and try to relax. Freaking out like this isn't going to help me at all.

Looking around, it's really obvious why I get so anxious every time I'm in here. The walls are greenish-yellow and very dirty. The steps are covered in filth, and the stairwell itself is narrower than I'd prefer.

And, there's one floor above me so God knows what's up there. It's after hours so it should be pretty quiet.

Or so I'm hoping.

Just need to sit here and wait. My watch says it's fifteen minutes past seven, so all I have to do is relax and allow this exercise to eliminate any sense of fear I have about this place.

This step is pretty hard to sit on. I think my ass is going to start hurting pretty soon so I'll see how long I can remain in one spot.

Screech.

What the hell?

Thump.

It sounds like someone upstairs has just stepped into the stairwell. No need to panic. Just need to breathe and not lose my cool.

Rat-a-tat.

Rat-a-tat.

Rat-a-tat.

Whoever it is, is coming down the stairwell. I can see the exit just fine from here but maybe I should get a little closer to it just in case. And I should mess with my phone so it looks like I'm not just hanging out in here. Don't want to be staring up when they come down.

Don't forget to pick up milk on your way home. Thanks.

Ok, I can answer her now so she doesn't think I'm ignoring her. My heart is beating pretty fast though. Shit. What if it's some kind of burglar? If he sees me and I see him, will he need to get rid of me because I can identify him to the police? Oh shit, this could be really bad, maybe I should—

"Excuse me."

He looks like a janitor. Thank goodness.

"No problem. Just getting ready to head home. Have a nice evening."

"You too."

Screech.

Thump.

Phew. That really stressed me out. What an idiot I am! It's just a janitor leaving after cleaning up one of the office buildings. I'm such a pussy.

Ok, time to relax and not worry. But maybe I'll sit closer to the exit anyway just to be sure I don't bump into any workaholics who've decided to stick around and work late.

Now that I've made my way down to the bottom of the stairwell, and I'm standing next to the exit, I'm noticing something that I've never seen before.

There are a pile of boxes lined up against the wall. That normally wouldn't be unusual but there's a big shadow behind them. So it seems like there's something back there that I can't see.

And the shadow is jagged.

I'm not sure it's such a good idea to go messing with things like that but I'm starting to get antsy. There are no loud noises or anything, but every so often I can hear the pipes jangling or a creak.

Need something else to focus on.

Ok, I'm going to get closer now. It's really not pleasant. There's a moldy smell in the air, and it's darker down here—closer to those boxes.

There seems to be a space behind them. But I'm going to have to move those boxes to see what's making that strange shadow. As I get closer to that weird thing, it may just be a trick of light but it seems like its shimmering along the edges.

This is nuts. There's no way there's something alive in that corner. I'm just tired and the smells are getting to me.

Still.

I need to move them. Not sure why or what is propelling me to do this. Just need to.

Ok. Here goes. I'm reaching out and ... something feels strange. The little hairs on my arm feel like they are standing up, and it's getting difficult to breathe.

The air must be off in here, because I'm starting to get dizzy. Need to shake it off. Need to focus.

Reaching out again, this time my fingers are connecting with the boxes that feel very dusty and old. Will really need to wash my hands as soon as I'm out of here. Maybe I'll use the sink in the office.

But that would mean having to go back up the stairs, and I don't really want to do that.

Almost there…

Wait! What the hell is that? Something's behind the boxes. I can see a dark shadow. And now the air feels cold.

Oh shit. What's that sound? It sounds like bees? A loud buzzing?

Can't breathe. Can't breathe. Can't stand. Can't see.

Can't …

Where am I?

I'm lying on the ground and my head is hurting. My stomach hurts, too, and the air smells.

Oh my God. I'm in the stairwell. That's right. The boxes. There was something behind the boxes.

Ok, going to try to sit up carefully, and then I'm going to get the hell out of here.

Ouch. Everything hurts really badly, and I really hope that I didn't break the phone when I fell. I might even have a concussion, because that's what happens when you hit your head really hard. Not sure how I passed out. I've never done that before.

The boxes are still there, up against the wall. It seems weird that I've fallen so close to the exit. Would've thought that a fall like that would've had me crash into the boxes since I was leaning in.

Strange.

Standing up isn't easy. My head hurts, and I feel dizzy. Nauseous, too. Better throw in the towel and will be taking the elevator from now on.

The door won't open.

I'm pushing and shoving against it, but for the first time since I started working in this god-forsaken building, the fucking door won't open.

What the hell? Is it locked? I keep pushing on the long silver bar that's supposed to let me out and it won't budge.

Starting to feel a little sweaty and nervous, but need to stay calm.

Remain calm. Take deep breaths and think.

Think!

Ok. If this door won't open then I will just use my special office pass to open the door on the second floor, and then I'll take the elevator down. No problem.

Easy-peasy.

Taking the stairs very carefully now. Since I've fallen, my balance feels a bit shaky, and I definitely don't need to stumble again. My wife's going to have enough questions for me when I come home all bedraggled and woozy.

Ok, I'm at the second floor. Let me just fish out my pass so I can open this door. It should be right in my pocket.

Hmm. That's strange. My pocket is empty. Let me try the other one.

That pocket is empty, too.

Maybe the pass fell on the floor when I blacked out?

Well, I have no choice. I've gotta go back down there and see if I can find it. It's definitely not on the floor here, and I don't see it lying on any of the steps.

Trying not to breathe too quickly, but I'm definitely starting to feel nervous. And on top of it, I feel like I've got to take a piss.

Probably just nerves. Got to get a handle on myself.

Heading back down. Back to the boxes.

It seems darker in here now. Not sure why. Maybe the lights dim as the hour gets later. It's going to make searching for my door pass more difficult. Whatever. I've gotta do what I've gotta do.

The floor is so dirty down here. There are small candy wrappers, dead bugs, and little dust bunnies. These have got to be old. And there's a dried-up lizard that looks like it's so old, it's practically mummified.

Where is that damned pass?

Maybe I dropped it behind the boxes?

Oh, shit. That's the last place I want to look. I passed out the last time I looked over there.

Not a good idea. Just have to keep looking. It's gotta be in here somewhere.

Buzz.

My cell phone!

Don't forget the milk. Going to bed early. Love you.

Shit. Now the wife's going to bed and she normally shuts off her phone when she sleeps. Should I call her and ask her to pick me up?

No. If I do that then she'll know I was lying and I'll never hear the end of it. Somehow I'll find my way out of this mess. And if it gets really bad, I'll call someone else. At least one of my friends should still be up. My wife always goes to bed really early because she's an early riser.

I like to stay up late and watch TV, maybe catch a bit of porn on the internet (Hey, I've been married a while, don't judge), or maybe play an old-school video game. Those are some great stress relievers.

Though right now, I'd give anything to be lying beside her, smelling her perfume, and maybe getting a bit frisky.

Or how about just finding a place to piss? This pressure's starting to become uncomfortable. Maybe I should find a place to just let it go. No one's here ...

Nah. That's gross. Gotta find the pass and get outta here. This whole idea was stupid, and I'm so nervous about this whole thing that I'm passing out cold. Not wise to keep this up.

Ok, where is that damned pass?

Maybe I should get a closer look at those boxes. I'm feeling a bit steadier now. Surely I'm not going to pass out a second time. It was probably just nerves.

What's that? There seems to be something sticking out of the back. It's dark but I think I can reach it.

It looks like a piece of paper and not my pass, but I'm still interested. Why would someone stick a note behind those boxes?

Taking a deep breath now and trying to steady myself. Hold it together, man. Don't let your nerves get the better of you. You're a fucking adult, and you don't believe in things like the boogeyman. Everything's going to be fine. Just take a deep breath in and reach ...

Got it!

Whew. That was stressful. I didn't see any dark shadows this time and managed to just reach out and pull that piece of paper out. Feeling kind of brave now and proud of myself.

Ok, let's open this thing up and see what it says.

Don't open the boxes. Fear the Dark one.

What the hell? Is this some kind of joke?

I've gotta read this thing again. This can't be happening.

Don't open the boxes. Fear the Dark one.

The Dark One? What is this? Who put this here? I can't

understand what's going on. Either I'm going crazy, or someone is seriously fucking with me. There's no such thing as ghosts, demons, or any of that shit. It's all something Hollywood has made up. It's fodder for reality TV. It's something that makes for a good novel.

But those things aren't real.

They can't be.

Then why am I still unwilling to open those boxes? And why am I so scared to push them away?

I need to find my door pass. If it's stuck behind those boxes then I have no choice. Fear or no fear, I've gotta push them aside and see if it somehow fell behind there when I blacked out.

Should I just forget this? Maybe there's someone still working on the third floor. It's just that it looks kinda scary and darker up there. Even though the lights are on up there, something doesn't feel right.

Not sure what to do.

I've been sitting here, crossing my legs, trying to not think about how badly I need a piss, and meanwhile, I still can't find that fucking door pass.

There's no more holding it in. I'm going to have to find a place to let this go.

Maybe I should just piss on the boxes. That would really anger "The Dark One" or whatever the hell the note is warning against.

Then again, maybe it's not such a good idea to create a mess near those boxes since I still think my pass is over there somehow. I'll have to find another place.

Somewhere that isn't as obvious as down here.

Starting to walk up the stairs again. I'm going to go all the way up to the third floor and see if I can find a place that isn't too obvious. Don't want to get arrested for this.

My steps are making such a loud sound in here. Didn't realize how quiet it is in this stairwell because I've been so concentrated on finding that pass. It also seems darker and stranger the more steps I climb.

Getting really nervous now. The lights up here don't look good. They're yellow and I can see little dead bugs trapped within them. Poor fuckers. They kind of seem like me. Trapped in this horrible place.

Ok, now I'm on the third floor. Just tried knocking on the door to see if by some miracle there's a person inside there working at nearly nine o'clock at night. No such luck, though.

The good news is that since I'm here at the top of the stairwell, there's a miniature corridor off to the side that is a perfect place for my piss.

And I've gotta go like a racehorse.

Aim, fire!

Whew! That felt good. There's quite a stream but it should be dried up by morning, and since no one from my job ever comes up here, I should be able to get away with this.

Just pulling up my pants and … whaaaa … ?

The lights up here have just gone out.

Oh, shit. Mother of God. This isn't good. It's really dark up here now.

I can see the lights downstairs, but it seems so far away. Christ. I need to get out of here.

Now.

Taking the stairs very slowly now. It appears that the lights near the second floor have also gone out. So the only lights that are on now are at the bottom level by the exit.

No worries. I'm fine. I can do this. My whole body is trembling now, and I'm feeling more than just a little uneasy at the moment. Actually, I'm feeling kind of scared. This all doesn't make sense. Maybe my piss set off some sort of alarm that causes the lights to go into "power-saving mode".

Whatever the case, I need to get down to the bottom level as quickly as possible.

What if the lights down there go out?

Can't think about that. Can't think about that. Just need to stay calm. Can't let my mind start racing out of control.

Breathe, man. Breathe.

I've finally made it to the exit.

Looking up, all I can see is darkness. It looks really bad. Like something out of a horror movie. Need to keep my eyes focused on the area around me.

And the boxes.

I've gotta move those boxes. My pass is back there.

I just know it.

Maybe I should call someone in the meanwhile. It couldn't hurt to call my friend Brad.

Brad is always calm and together. Nothing ever affects him, and he always takes everything in stride. Like the time we got into a car accident. We were both in the car when it was rear-ended by some teenage girl who was texting and driving. Her excuse was that she was in a big fight with her idiot boyfriend and that's why she took her eyes off the road and texted instead of noticing that the traffic had slowed due to an accident. She was still texting when her car hit us. Hard.

We both flew forward but thankfully the car ahead of us

was stopped so it essentially halted our movement.

It was not pretty—rear-ended and then slamming into the car in front of us.

But Brad emerged calm and collected. Neither of us were seriously hurt, but he was the calm one.

I, on the other hand, was shocked at first, and then furious— flying out of the car and screaming at the teenager.

"What the hell is wrong with you? You could've fucking killed us? Are you crazy?"

Part of me still wonders if I would've actually assaulted that teenager if Brad hadn't pulled me back and helped me get a hold of myself.

He saved me that day.

I can make bad decisions. It's just part of my personality.

Time to call him.

Pulling out my cellphone and not happy with what I see. The face is dark. Like the battery has died.

How is that possible? Wasn't it working just a moment ago? Did I forget to charge it?

Wonderful. Now, I have no way to contact anyone, and if I can't find that pass I'll be stuck here until morning. And how will explain that to my wife? And to my boss or co-workers?

Oh, no. Can't tell them the truth. Will have to lie, and say that I came back to the office to pick something up, and somehow I lost my pass and got stuck in the stairwell.

This fucking stairwell.

I hate this stairwell.

Man. I need to find a way out of this. The idea of spending the night here amongst the dust and bugs and those … boxes.

This is ridiculous. I should just man-up and move those damned things out of the way.

And anyway, the note warns against opening them. That's not my plan at all. I'm just going to move them out of the way so that I can look behind them.

Not a big deal, right?

Exactly.

So why are my hands shaking, and why does my stomach hurt like hell?

I don't believe in ghosts.

I don't believe in ghosts.

Stepping forward now and reaching out. Just need to bat those boxes out of the way.

Here we go.

One...

Two...

Three...

Whack!

Oh, shit. Oh, shit. That was scary as hell, but I'm still here and conscious and nothing bad happened.

The boxes are lying all over the ground though, and I still can't see if my pass is lying amongst them.

Buzz, buzz.

There's that sound again. I can't tell where it's coming from. Maybe it's just the air-conditioning kicking on.

Just ignore it. There's nothing there. Focus on the task at hand.

The boxes aren't the same size. They looked that way when I was standing farther away, but now that they're all scattered along the floor, it looks like there are some big ones and some small ones.

And they all look like they're sealed with packing tape. That's a good thing because I certainly don't plan on opening any of them.

Except maybe that one.

There's this little box not far from my feet, and it's odd. There's this brownish stain on it that seems to be spreading along the surface.

And look, it's stained the floor, too.

Brown? It can't be blood, but what if it's something toxic? I really shouldn't be messing with any of these boxes, but I'm curious.

Where is my pass? Is it lying amongst these things? I'm not happy having to mess with these boxes any more than I have to, but there are so many of them and some are so large that it would be easy to conceal a small card-sized door pass.

Shit. Some of these are hard and not easy to push out of the way.

And there are still some stacked up against the wall.

Buzz, buzz.

What is that noise? That's the second time I've heard it. It sounds like insects. Damn, I hope there isn't some strange swarm of bugs in here. That's all I need. And I'm allergic to bee stings. Severely allergic. Wouldn't that just be the kicker? Get stuck in here all night, only to get stung by a fucking bee.

That's not going to happen. I'm going to find my way out.

One way or the other.

It's surprising how many boxes are down here. I mean, if there was something valuable in them, why would they be left out for anyone to take?

I keep looking at the smaller box. For some reason, it just seems like there's something damaged in there. That brown stain keeps spreading, too.

What is that? Oh my God. The light down here is starting to flicker too. Dear Lord, please don't leave me here in the dark.

Ok, that's it. Time to get serious about finding my door pass.

Pushing all the boxes around now, as fast as I can. The light above is flickering regularly now, and it is clear that I don't have much time before I am stuck in the dark.

Wait. That box with the stain on it has something printed on the side. It is a small label, but I think I can read it.

SURPLUS DOOR PASSES

What? This is too good to be true.

Someone has to be messing with me.

The box is stained, looks sticky, and I can't imagine that there's door passes in there.

But what if there are?

Shit. The note is warning me not to open this thing or I will evoke some sort of rage from "The Dark One". But that's all bull, isn't it? If I can get a door pass, then I will leave and never speak of this night again.

It will be like it never happened.

Nothing's going to attack me.

Ghosts don't exist.

Ok, to hell with this. I'm going to open the box.

It looks like it's sealed shut with tape, so I'm going to need to use my keys to slice it open. Better put my phone on the floor while I do this—it's useless anyway.

Here goes, starting to slice. Man, it isn't easy to get this thing open, but I'd better do this quickly because the light is flickering even worse now.

One more slice and I think I've got this …

Woah. It's open. Just need to pull back the flaps and …

Shit! It's full of bees. Crap! That brown stuff was honey! Oh my God. The buzzing noise was coming from inside these boxes. Now they're all buzzing.

They're all full of bees!

Can't think. Can't breathe.

Oh, shit.

The remaining lights have just gone out.

Now, I'm in the dark with bees all over the place and no way out.

Wait! My phone is lighting up. There's a message on it! I'm saved! I can call for help and all I've gotta do is steer clear of those things until someone arrives. What a blessing.

Buzz, buzz.

Let me carefully pick it up so that I don't disturb the bees. I can feel them flying all around me now.

Oh, please, dear Lord, let me get out of here in one piece.

What does the message say?

Hi, Sweetheart. By now, you should have picked up the milk, right?

They always say you should have some Milk and Honey. So here's my gift to you. Hope you enjoy. The Dark One is waiting. And I'm not. Take a hard look around. In a few short moments, you won't be able to see anything anymore. Love you bunches.

What? Oh my God. This isn't happening. I mean, I know I haven't always been the best husband, and maybe I should have tried harder in our marriage, and maybe I left out the cheating thing that she caught me doing. But marriage is hard, and work is so stressful and we've been on autopilot and everything has been better lately.

How could she do this to me?

No. I'm going to find my way out. There's no such thing as ghosts, and when I find her—I'll leave her with nothing. I'll divorce her ass, and then sue her for harassment and then ... ouch!

I've been bitten.

I've been bitten.

Holy shit. What am I going to do? I can already feel my heart pounding. Need to get out of here or I'll die of asphyxiation.

Cough.

My phone's dead again so I can't call for help, but maybe if I bang on the door someone will hear me.

Bang.

Bang.

Bang.

Help! Can anyone hear me? Help!

The light is flickering again. No! Stop flickering!

Shit! It's gone out entirely. I can't see anything.

Cough.

Cough.

I've gotta ... get out of here somehow ...

What? I feel something ...

Cough.

Cough.

Cough.

Having trouble breathing. Can't think. There's something here. I'm not alone. There is something here.

What is that? What is that thing breathing so heavily? Is it me?

Just bumped into something. It is prickly and smells bad. It just groaned in my ear.

Is there something here? The Dark One? Or am I just hallucinating?

My throat is closing up. I can't breathe. Starting to wheeze. Throat is closing up. Chest hurts.

Falling to the floor.

No. Please no. Please.

Cough.

Cough.
Cough.
Cough.
Rattle.

About the Author

Sara Brooke is an Amazon bestselling author of horror, paranormal romance, and suspense fiction.

A lifelong avid reader of all things scary, Sara's childhood dream was to write books that make readers sleep with their lights on. She hopes that isn't too troubling for the thousands of readers worldwide who have purchased her books.

Sara has been published alongside horror legends Clive Barker and John Carpenter. She has written eight novels and numerous short stories. Her series "The Bloodmane Chronicles" is in development for a potential cable series.

Sara resides in beautiful South Florida. She can be reached via her website at www.sarabrooke.com. Sara welcomes feedback and questions from readers.

Curious about other Crossroad Press books?
Stop by our site:
http://store.crossroadpress.com
We offer quality writing
in digital, audio, and print formats.

Enter the code FIRSTBOOK
to get 20% off your first order from our store!
Stop by today!